The dark blue of his eyes intensified, holding hers in a lock that made something inside her belly tilt and then spill.

'You're scared.'

Aiesha sent her tongue out in a quick darting movement to moisten her lips. 'Let me go, James.'

'I have a little forfeit to collect first.'

Something dropped off a shelf in her stomach. 'Forfeit?'

He spread his hands through the mane of her hair, his gaze moving from her eyes to her mouth in a slow and mesmerising fashion. 'You remember? Now I get to kiss you. Fair's fair.'

She affected a sneer but was pretty sure it was wide of the mark. 'Is that meant to be a punishment?'

'Why don't we find out?' he said, tugging her against him, and his mouth came down over hers.

From as soon as **Melanie Milburne** could pick up a pen she knew she wanted to write. It was when she picked up her first Mills & Boon® at seventeen that she realised she wanted to write romance. After being distracted for a few years by meeting and marrying her own handsome hero, surgeon husband Steve, and having two boys, plus completing a Masters of Education and becoming a nationally ranked athlete (masters swimming), she decided to write. Five submissions later she sold her first book and is now a multi-published, bestselling, award-winning *USA TODAY* author. In 2008 she won the Australian Readers' Association most popular category/series romance, and in 2011 she won the prestigious Romance Writers of Australia R*BY award.

Melanie loves to hear from her readers via her website, www.melaniemilburne.com.au or on Facebook: www.facebook.com/pages/Melanie-Milburne/351594482609.

Recent titles by the same author:

NEVER GAMBLE WITH A CAFFARELLI
 (Those Scandalous Caffarellis)
NEVER UNDERESTIMATE A CAFFARELLI
 (Those Scandalous Caffarellis)
NEVER SAY NO TO A CAFFARELLI
 (Those Scandalous Caffarellis)
HIS FINAL BARGAIN

**Did you know these are also available as eBooks?
Visit www.millsandboon.co.uk**

AT NO MAN'S COMMAND

BY
MELANIE MILBURNE

**MORAY COUNCIL
LIBRARIES &
INFO.SERVICES**

20 37 31 30	
Askews & Holts	
RF RF	

AT NO MAN'S
COMMAND

To Nadine and Regan Drew.
Thanks for your friendship
and all the fun memories we share.
May there be many more to come! xx

CHAPTER ONE

AIESHA HAD BEEN at Lochbannon a week without a single whisper in the press about her whereabouts. But then, who would have thought of hunting her down in the Highlands of Scotland in the home of the woman whose marriage she had effectively destroyed ten years ago?

It was the perfect hideaway, and the fact that Louise Challender had been called away to visit a sick friend abroad meant Aiesha had had the place to herself for the last couple of days. And, being the dead of winter, there was not even a housekeeper or a gardener to disturb her idyll.

Bliss.

She closed her eyes and, tilting her head back, breathed in the ice in the air as fresh flakes of snow began to fall. The soft press of each snowflake was like a caress against her skin. After the traffic fumes and incessant noise and activity of Las Vegas, the cold, fresh, quiet Highland air was like breathing in an elixir, bringing her jaded senses back to zinging life.

Being up here on her own where no one could find her was like coming off a stage. Stepping out of a costume. Undressing the part of Vegas showgirl. She could feel it falling away from her like a heavy cloak. Up here she could take her game face off. The flirty vamp face. The face that told everyone she was perfectly happy singing in a gentlemen's club because the tips were great and she had the days free to shop, hang out by the pool or get a spray tan.

Up here in the Highlands she could relax. Regroup. Get in touch with nature.

Revisit her dreams…

The only hiccup was the dog.

Aiesha could babysit cats, no problem. Cats were pretty easy to take care of. She just filled their dish with biscuits and cleaned out their litter tray, if they had one. She didn't have to pat them or get close to them. Most cats were pretty aloof, which suited her just fine.

Dogs were different. Dogs wanted to get close to you. To bond with you. To love you.

To trust you to keep them safe.

Aiesha glanced down at the limpid brown eyes of the golden retriever sitting at her feet with slavish devotion, its tail brushing against the carpet of snow like a feathered fan.

The memory of another pair of trusting brown eyes stabbed at her heart like a knitting needle. Eyes that still haunted her, even though so many years had passed. She pushed back the thick sleeve of her coat and looked at the underside of her wrist where the blue-and-red ink of her tattoo was a vivid and permanent reminder of her failure to keep her one and only best friend safe.

Aiesha swallowed the monkey wrench of guilt in her

throat and frowned down at the dog. 'Why can't you take yourself for a walk? It's not as if you need me to show you the way. There aren't any fences to stop you.' She made a shooing motion with her hand. 'Go on. Go for a run. Go chase a rabbit or a stoat or something.'

The dog continued to look at her with that unblinking stare, a soft little 'play with me' whine coming from its throat. Aiesha blew out a breath of resignation and began trudging in the direction of the forest that fringed the stately Highland home. 'Come on, then, you stupid mutt. But I'm only going as far as the river. It looks like this snow's going to set in for the night.'

James Challender drove through the snow-encrusted wrought-iron gates of Lochbannon as evening folded in. The secluded estate was spectacular in any season but in winter it turned into a wonderland. The Gothic-style mansion with its turrets and spires looked like something out of a children's fairy tale. The frozen water in the fountain in front of the house looked like a Renaissance ice sculpture with delicate icicles hanging down like centuries-old stalactites. The thick forest that backed on to the estate was coated in pure white snow, the rolling fields were also thickly carpeted, and the air was so sharp and clean and cold it burned his nostrils as he drew it in.

The lights were on in the house, which meant the housekeeper, Mrs McBain, had generously postponed her annual holiday to look after Bonnie while his mother visited her friend, who had suffered an accident in outback Australia. James had offered to look after the dog but his mother had insisted via a hurried text before she boarded her flight that it was all organised and not to worry. Why his mother couldn't put her dog in boarding kennels like everyone else did was beyond him. It wasn't as if she couldn't afford it. He'd made sure she was well provided for after the divorce from his father.

Lochbannon was a little large for an older single woman with only a dog for company and a handful of staff, but he had wanted to give his mother a safe haven, a place that was totally unconnected to her former life as Clifford Challender's wife.

Although he had insisted the estate was in his mother's name, James liked to spend the occasional week up in the Highlands away from the fast lane of London, which was why he'd decided to come up in spite of his mother's assurances that Bonnie was well taken care of.

This was the one place he could focus without distractions. A week working here was worth a month in his busy London office. He liked the solitude, the peace and tranquillity of being alone, without people needing him to fix something, do something or be something.

Here he could let his shoulders down and relax. Here he could think. Clear his head of the stress of managing a company that was still suffering the effects of his father's mishandling of projects and clients.

Lochbannon was also one of the few places where he could escape the intrusive spotlight of the press. The repercussions of his father's profligate lifestyle had spread across his own life like an indelible stain. The newshounds were always on the lookout for a scandal to prove their theory of 'like father, like son.'

Even before he turned off the engine he heard the sound of Bonnie's welcoming bark. He smiled as he walked to the front door. Maybe his mother was right about her precious dog being too sensitive to leave with strangers. Besides, he had to admit there was something rather homely and comfortable about an enthusiastic canine greeting.

The door opened before he could put his key in the lock and a pair of wide grey eyes blinked at him in outraged shock, as if suddenly finding a prowler on the doorstep instead of the postman. 'What the hell are *you* doing here?'

James's hand fell away from the door. His body went stiff as if the snow falling behind him had frozen him to the spot. *Aiesha Adams*. The infamous, lethally gorgeous, impossibly sexy and outrageously wild Aiesha Adams. 'I believe that's supposed to be my line,' he said when he could locate his voice.

At a casual glance there was nothing outstanding about her features. Dressed in a loose-fitting boyfriend sweater and yoga pants and without make-up, she looked like your average girl next door. Midlength chestnut hair that was neither curly nor straight but somewhere in between. Skin that was clear and unlined apart from a couple of tiny scars that were either from chickenpox or the site of a picked pimple, one on the left side of her forehead and one just below her right cheekbone. She was of average height and of slim build, the result of lucky genes rather than effort, he surmised.

For a moment—a brief moment—she looked fifteen years old again.

But look a little closer and the unusual colour of her eyes was nothing short of arresting. Breath-snatching. Storm and smoke and shadows swirled in their depths.

The shape of her mouth had the power to render a man speechless. That lush, ripe mouth was pure sin. The bee-stung fullness, the youthfulness, and the vermillion borders so beautifully aligned it physically hurt to look and not touch.

What was she doing here? Had she broken in?

What if someone found out she was here…*with him*? His heart galloped ahead a few beats. What if the press found out? What if Phoebe found out?

Aiesha's chin came up to that don't-mess-with-me height James had seen her do so well in the past, her body posture morphing from schoolgirl to sultry, defiant tart in a blink. 'Your mother invited me.'

His mother? James's frown was so tight it made his forehead hurt. What was going on? His mother's rushed text message hadn't mentioned anything about Aiesha. Not. One. Word. Why would his mother invite the girl who'd caused so much heartbreak and mayhem in the past? It didn't make sense.

'Rather magnanimous of her under the circumstances, is it not?' he said. 'Has she locked up her jewellery and all the silver?'

Her eyes flashed gunmetal-grey fire at him. 'Is anyone with you?'

'I hate to repeat myself, but I believe that's what *I'm* supposed to be asking you.' James closed the door on the chilly air but, in doing so, it made the sudden silence and the space between them far too intimate.

Being intimate—in any sense of the word—with Aiesha Adams was dangerous. He dared not think about it. Would *not* think about it. Being in the same country as her was reputation suicide, let alone in the same house. She oozed sex appeal. She wore it like a slinky coat, slipping in and out of it whenever she felt the urge. Every movement she made was pure seductress. How many men had fallen for that lithe body and that Lolita mouth? Even with that smoky glower and that upthrust chin she still managed to look sex kittenish. He could feel the thrum of his blood in his veins, the sudden rush of sexual awareness that was as shocking to him as it was unwelcome.

He bent down to ruffle Bonnie's ears to distract himself and was rewarded with a whimper and a lavish licking. At least someone was pleased to see him.

'Did anyone follow you here?' Aiesha asked. 'The press? Journalists? Anyone?'

James straightened from ruffling the dog's ears to give her a sardonic look. 'Running away from another scandal, are we?'

Her lips tightened, her eyes burning with the dislike she had always assaulted him with. 'Don't pretend you don't know. It's been in every paper and newsfeed.'

Was there anyone who *didn't* know? The news of her affair with a married politician in the U.S. had gone viral. James had pointedly ignored it, or tried to. But then some unscrupulous newshound had unearthed Aiesha's role in the break-up of his parents' marriage. It had only been a sentence or two and not every paper or newsfeed ran with it, but the shame and embarrassment he had been trying to put behind him for a decade was back with a vengeance.

But what else could he expect? Aiesha was a wild child who attracted scandal and had been from the moment his mother had brought her home from the back streets of London as a teenage runaway. She was a smart-mouthed little guttersnipe who deliberately created negative drama, even for the people who tried to help her. His mother had been badly let down by Aiesha's disreputable behaviour in the past, which was why he was puzzled that she had allowed her to come and stay now. Why would his mother invite the unscrupulous girl who had stolen not only heirloom jewellery from her, but tried to steal her husband from her, as well?

James shrugged off his coat to hang it in the cupboard in the hall. 'Married men are a particular obsession of yours, are they not?'

He felt the stab of those grey eyes drilling between his shoulder blades. He felt the sudden kick of his pulse. He got a thrill out of seeing her rattled by him. He was the only person she couldn't hide her true colours from. She was a true chameleon, changing to serve her interests, laying on the charm when it suited her, reeling in her next victim, enjoying the game of slaying yet another heart and wallet.

But he was immune. He'd seen her for what she was right from the start. She might have got rid of her East End accent and chain-store clothes, but underneath she was a pickpocket whose aim in life was to sleep her way to the top. Her latest victim was a U.S. senator whose career and marriage were unravelling as a result. The press had captured a damning shot of her leaving his suite at the Vegas hotel where she worked as a lounge singer.

'No one must know I'm here,' she said. 'Do you understand? No one.'

James turned from neatly arranging the sleeves of his coat to face her. She was still looking at him with hatred but something else moved in her gaze, a flicker of uncertainty, or was it fear? She quickly disguised it, however. She jutted her chin and flattened those delectably full lips. Her mouth had always fascinated him. Ripe and soft and full, a mouth built for sin and sex and seduction. There was nothing innocent about her mouth or her body. She was a five-foot-eight knockout package of sinuous catlike curves that could wrap around a man until he was strangled by his need of her.

And she knew it.

James moved past her to stride to the warmth of the sitting room. Thinking about that mouth was a bad move. He could practically *feel* those plump lips clasped around him, drawing on him until he went weak at the knees. He suppressed a shudder of traitorous desire. He would *not* think about that mouth. He would *not* think about that body. He would *not* think of the lust that burned inside him.

'No one will find you here because you're not staying.'

She followed him into the sitting room, her bare feet padding over the Persian carpet like the paws of a light-footed lioness. 'You can't throw me out. This is your mother's house, not yours.' She stood with her arms folded across her chest, looking exactly like she had a decade ago, all pouty, sulky teenager even though she was now twenty-five years old.

He let his gaze run over her in a leisurely sweep as if inspecting a cheap and tawdry item he had no intention of buying. 'Pack your bags and get out.'

She slitted her eyes like a wildcat staring down a wolf. 'I'm *not* leaving.'

James felt his blood skip and then roar through his veins. It thickened in his groin, reigniting the embers of a fire that had never quite been extinguished. He hated himself for it. He saw it as a weakness. It reduced him to the baseness of a wild animal with no other instinct than to mate with whatever willing female was available.

He wasn't cut from the same low-quality cloth as his father. He could control his impulses. Aiesha had tried her seduction routine on him ten years ago but he hadn't taken the bait.

And he wasn't going to take it now.

'I'm expecting a guest,' he said.

'Who?'

'The woman I intend to marry is joining me at the weekend. You'll be decidedly de trop.'

She laughed out loud, even going so far as to bend over double to hold her sides as if he'd told her the most humorous of jokes. 'You mean to say you've actually *asked* that stuck-up frozen-faced heiress who doesn't do anything but spend Daddy's money on the High Street to marry you?'

James ground his teeth so hard he thought he'd have

to take his meals through a straw for the rest of his life. 'Phoebe's the patron of several well-known charities.'

Aiesha was still giggling like a naughty schoolgirl. It made the base of his spine tighten like a bowstring. How like her to mock the most important decision of his life. He had chosen his future bride after lengthy consideration. Phoebe Trentonfield had her own money, which meant he could rule out the gold-digging factor. It had plagued him for most of his adult life, trying to find a partner who wanted him for himself instead of his money. It was the first box he wanted ticked. He was thirty-three years old. He wanted to settle down. He wanted to build a stable home life—like the one he'd thought he had until his father's affairs had come to light. He wanted his mother to enjoy the experience of having grandchildren. He wanted someone who was content to be a traditional wife so he could rebuild the Challender empire his father had so recklessly frittered away. He wanted stability and predictability instead of scandal and chaos. His father was the impulsive one. Not him. He knew what he wanted and was determined and disciplined enough to get it and keep it.

Aiesha gave him a goading look. 'What's she going to say when she finds out you're here with me?'

His molars went down another couple of millimetres. 'She's not going to find out because you're leaving first thing in the morning.'

She hitched one of her hips in a model-like pose, a teasing smile still lurking around the corners of her mouth. 'So you're not going to be a big old meanie and throw me out in the snow on my toosh tonight, then?'

He wanted to bury her in the snow, at least ten feet deep so he wouldn't be tempted to touch her. And the less he thought about her curvy little toosh the better. How was he going to get her out of here? He could hardly send her packing at this time of night, with the roads so slippery and treacherous. He had only just made it through from the main road himself. The nearest village had a bed and breakfast but it was currently closed for the winter. The closest hotel was a half hour drive away…an hour in these conditions. 'Does your car have snow chains?' he asked.

'I didn't bring a car. Your mother picked me up from the airport in Edinburgh.'

What was his mother thinking? This was getting crazier by the minute. He hadn't known his mother had been in contact with Aiesha over the years. What was she thinking bringing the daughter of the devil back into her life?

Was this a set-up? A practical joke?

Surely not… How on earth could it be? His mother had insisted he not worry about the dog. Surely she knew how dangerous it would be to put Aiesha in the same house as him. She was a ticking time bomb. She courted trouble. She craved attention from anyone wearing trousers, making it her mission to get them out of them as fast as she could. She was ruthless and shameless and as sexy as a pin-up girl. *Damn it.* 'Right, well, I'll drive you back to the airport first thing in the morning,' he said. 'Your little stint as dog- and house-sitter is over.'

She sashayed over to him, deliberately trailing one

of her fingertips along one of the whitened tendons on
the back of one of his clenched fists. 'Loosen up, James.
You're as wound up as a tight spring. If you need an
outlet for all that pressure—' she batted her impossibly
long eyelashes at him '—just call me, OK?'

James forced himself to endure the electric shock of
her touch without flinching. He forced himself not to
look at her mouth, where the tip of her pink tongue had
left a moistly glistening trail. He forced himself not to
slam her against the nearest wall and slake the fireball
of his lust by plunging into her hot, wet warmth and
doing what he'd always wanted to do to her. Every cell
in his body was vibrating with need, and what sickened
him the most was she damn well knew it. 'Get the freaking hell out of my sight.'

Her eyes glinted with devilment. 'I love it when a
man talks dirty to me.' She gave an exaggerated little
shiver that made her braless breasts jiggle beneath her
sweater. 'It makes me come in a flash.'

James curled his fingers so tightly into his palms he
felt every one of their joints protest. 'Be ready at seven.
Understood?'

She gave him another sultry little smile that sent
another scorching flare to his groin. 'You can't get rid
of me that easily. Didn't you hear the weather report
for tonight?'

A fist of panic clutched at his insides. He'd heard
it in the car half an hour ago but back then he'd welcomed the thought of a blizzard snowing him in for a
few days so he could put the final touches to the draw-

ings on the Sherwood project before Phoebe joined him at the weekend.

He glared at Aiesha with such intense loathing he could feel it burning through his eyeballs like hot pokers. 'You planned this, didn't you?'

She tossed the length of her glossy chestnut hair back over one of her shoulders as she laughed that spine-fizzing laugh again. 'You think I've got that much power that I can manipulate the weather to suit me? You flatter me, James.'

He sucked in a breath as she moved to the stairs with her swinging hip gait. Carnal lust roared in his body but he wasn't going to let her win this. They could be snowed in for a month and he would still resist her.

He would *not* give in.

He. Would. Not. Give. In.

CHAPTER TWO

AIESHA LEANED BACK against the door of her bedroom and let out a long ragged breath. Her heart was still flapping like a loosely tied flag in a gale force wind. This couldn't be happening.

James Challender wasn't just a press magnet. He was press superglue. Where he went the press followed, especially if anyone got a heads-up on his upcoming engagement. He was one of London's most eligible bachelors—the epitome of the Prize Catch. Every woman under the age of fifty panted after him. He was suave, sophisticated. Not a playboy like his father, but a classy specimen of modern sexy corporate man. Before she knew it, her sanctuary would be invaded by hundreds of journalists and prying cameras, hoping to get the latest scoop on him.

She would be hunted down. Found. Exposed. Mocked. Shamed.

The scandal she was trying to distance herself from would arrive on the doorstep. The shame of being at the centre of something so sordid wasn't new to her. She'd spent most of her life attracting scandals, encouraging them, relishing in them for the attention they gave her, which made up for the lack of attention she'd received as a child.

But that chapter was supposed to be over.

She wanted to put that part of her life behind her and move forward. The meeting with Antony Smithson— aka Antony Gregovitch—was supposed to have been her big break. The chance to get out of the club scene and nail the recording contract she'd longed for since she was a little kid singing into her hairbrush in front of a mottled mirror in a council flat. Instead, she'd found out he wasn't a music producer at all. He'd lied to her from the moment he'd sat down to listen to her sing through her shift. He'd come night after night, staying to talk to her between breaks, buying her drinks, telling her how beautiful her voice was, how talented she was. Fool that she was, she had sucked it all up and basked in his praise.

That was what angered her the most—the fact she hadn't seen through him. How could she have been so gullible, especially the way she'd been dragged up by a bunch of tricksters and sham artists? He hadn't been the handsome prince to rescue her from a life of singing to people who were too drunk to even listen to a word of her lyrics. He was a married man with a wife and family who was looking for a bit of cheap fun on the side.

Now she was painted as a heartless home-wrecker and her chance to prove she was so much more than a nightclub one-trick pony was over. She had no record-ing contract. She didn't even have a job. Antony's wife's smear campaign had seen to that. There wasn't a club in Vegas—possibly in the entire world—that would take her on now.

And now she had to deal with James High-and-Mighty Challender.

In spite of everything, Aiesha couldn't help a tiny smile of self-congratulation. She knew exactly how hard to tug on his chain. She had practised her moves on him when she was fifteen. He had a little more self-control than his sleazeball of a father, but she hated him just as much. But then she hated all men, especially superrich ones who thought they could have anyone they wanted just by fanning open their wallet. Sexually they were OK, quite useful for a bit of fun now and again, but as people? No. She hadn't met any she respected as a person. The men in her life had always let her down. Tricked her. Betrayed her. Exploited her.

James Challender might think he could control her but she wasn't leaving Lochbannon on his say-so. His mother had given her permission to stay for as long as she liked. She wasn't going to be pushed around by a stuffed shirt whose vocabulary didn't possess the words fun or spontaneity. He was a nitpicking, timekeeping workaholic who got antsy if the cushions on the sofa weren't neatly aligned.

And as for his so-called fiancée…what a joke! They deserved each other. Phoebe whatever-her-name-was did nothing but smile inanely at the cameras, showing off her perfect toothpaste-commercial smile and her perfect clothes and her perfect figure while her equally pampered and perfect parents pumped up her trust fund.

Bitch.

Aiesha tapped her fingers against her lips. Maybe there was a way for her to get this unexpected little speed bump to work in her favour. Why would anyone think she was hooking her claws into a boring old married politician back in Vegas when someone as staggeringly gorgeous as James Challender was spending the week cloistered with her up here in the Highlands?

She reached for her phone with a mischievous grin. *Twitter, here I come!*

James hadn't been able to get through to his mother but he left a message. A rather stern one, lecturing her on the pitfalls of harbouring a headline-grabbing harlot who was sure to pilfer the silver or trash the place with a wild party in her absence.

He rubbed a golf-ball knot of tension in his neck as he looked at the steady fall of snow outside the library window. For once the weather forecasters were spot on. It was snowing a blizzard and any chance of leaving now—let alone in the morning—was well and truly out of the question.

He dropped his hand back down by his side with a whooshing sigh. Thank God no one knew he was here with Aiesha. *Yet.* He'd checked on his phone earlier to see if anyone had tracked her down but so far they hadn't. The Vegas scandal was still generating plenty of comments, most of them unflattering to her on her part in destroying a perfectly respectable man's career and marriage. Personally, he thought some of the comments were a little harsh. Surely the man in question had to take some responsibility?

But then he thought of her little seductive moves downstairs. She was one hell of a temptation even the purest of monks would find hard to resist. His body was still reverberating with shockwaves of unbridled lust. She did it for the sport of it. It amused her to tempt and tease. It was a game, a competition to see who had the most willpower. He'd won that battle a decade ago. He'd been proud of his strength of will, but back then she'd been a kid. Now she was an adult and twice as dangerous. She'd had years to perfect her art of playing the courtesan.

James clenched and unclenched his hands. His skin was still burning from her sizzling touch and nothing he did would quell it. He had never thought of himself as a hedonistic sensualist. He enjoyed sex but there was an element to it that had always disturbed him. The closeness that came with sex and the out of control aspect made him uneasy. The idea of being vulnerable and at the mercy of another unnerved him and meant he always kept his passion on a tight leash. He was by no means prudish but he was uneasy with the thought of giving in to primal urges without thought of the consequences.

Like his father, for instance, moving from one relationship to another with a series of totally unsuitable women. His latest mistress was barely legal, yet another wannabe starlet looking for a sugar daddy to give her a good time. The shallowness of his father was a constant irritation to him. A constant embarrassment. A constant source of shame. He hated the assumption he was like his father because they shared the same features.

He wasn't the same.

He had drive and ambition where his father had none. He had focus and discipline. He cared about the company. He cared about the people who worked in the company.

Hard work and responsibility weren't words James associated with his father. Born to wealth, which he'd proceeded to dispense with as soon as it was bequeathed to him, Clifford Challender had all but destroyed the coffers and the reputation of the architectural empire James's grandfather had worked so hard to build.

Now the baton was in James's hand and he wasn't going to let it go until he had the company back where it belonged, up there with the top ten architectural firms in the country.

The Sherwood project was a pivotal step towards that dream. The multimillion-pound redesign of Howard Sherwood's London home and his Paris townhouse was small change compared to other projects the influential and well-connected businessman could send James's way. If James secured this contract then his dream of designing luxury environmentally friendly accommodation in select wilderness areas across the globe would be one step closer. It wasn't just the money that motivated him. The project was true to his values as an architect. He wanted to leave a legacy of buildings that enhanced the environments in which they were set, not exploiting or desecrating or destroying them. And it would be one step closer to proving he was nothing like his wastrel father.

Bonnie lifted her golden head off the carpet at James's feet and gave a soft whine. 'You want to go outside, old girl?' he asked. 'Come on. It looks like your babysitter's walked off the job.'

The snow was already up to his calves and the wind was howling like a dervish but fortunately the dog didn't take too long about her business. James dusted the snow off his shoulders as he came back in the back door leading off the kitchen. The back of his neck prickled when he saw Aiesha leaning in an indolent manner against the kitchen counter, her lushly youthful mouth curved upwards in a mocking tilt. 'I hope you're not expecting me to cook dinner for you.'

'I wouldn't dream of putting you to the tedious inconvenience of doing something for someone else.'

He opened the fridge and inspected the contents. The usual suspects were there—eggs, yoghurt, milk and cheese, vegetables in the crisper and Bonnie's meat in a Tupperware container.

'You can feed the dog now you're here,' Aiesha said. 'And you can walk her. I'm not going to freeze my butt off just because that overweight mutt needs to take a leak every five minutes.'

He closed the fridge to look at her again. 'So how *are* you going to earn your keep?'

Her grey eyes glinted as the tilt of her lush mouth went a little higher. 'Any suggestions?'

A rocket blast of blood slammed into his groin at her saucy look. His mind filled with images of his body rocking against hers, pumping, thrusting, exploding. He clenched his teeth, fighting the demons of desire that plagued him whenever she was within touching distance. She knew the effect she had on him. Knew it and relished it. But he wondered if it was not so much a game now but a tactic to get rid of him.

The more he thought about it, the more likely it seemed. She had hidden herself away from the press in the last place anyone would think to find her. His coming here had jeopardised the safety of her hideout.

He had no time for the press, especially since his father's exploits had sullied the family name so lamentably, but his own profile had attracted a fair bit of interest over the years. He had been in the gossip pages more than he wanted to be, but that came with the territory of being considered one of Britain's most eligible bachelors. The announcement of his engagement would bring a storm of interest his way, which was clearly something Aiesha was keen to avoid while she was holed up here with him.

James curled his top lip at her. 'You think I'd get mixed up with a cheap little two-bit tramp like you?'

She sent her smoky eyes over his body from head to foot, lingering on his groin for a heart-stopping, pulse-thundering pause, before re-engaging with his gaze with a mischievous twinkle of her own. She lifted the smartphone she was holding in one hand, tapping one of her slender fingers on the screen. 'You might want to check in with your fiancée. Fill her in on your current location and choice of company before she hears it from another source.'

James felt every hair on his scalp tighten at the roots as if being tugged out by tiny elves. But, before he could get his mouth open to speak, his phone started to ring. He took it out of his pocket, his stomach dropping as Phoebe's image came up on the screen. 'Hi, Phoebe, I was just about to—'

'You bastard!'

'It's not what you think,' he said, thinking on his feet and not doing a particularly good job of it. 'She's practically my…er…adopted sister. My mother is supposed to be here but she got called away at the—'

'Oh, for God's sake. Don't take me for a complete and utter fool. It's all over social media. You're having a fling with a—' the disgust and incredulity was starkly apparent in Phoebe's tone '—*a Vegas lounge singer?*'

James blinked. His heart thudded. His brow broke out in a hot prickling sweat. The Sherwood project flashed before his eyes. All the tricky negotiations he'd gone through to nail the pitch, all the work he'd done—hours and hours, weeks and weeks, months and months of his time—would be for naught if the ultra-conservative Howard Sherwood heard about this before he could explain the circumstances. 'Listen, I can explain everyth—'

'It's over,' Phoebe said. 'Not that I was going to say yes if you ever happened to get around to proposing to me. Daddy was right about you. He said the apple never falls far from the tree and your family tree is particularly rotten. You're just like your jailbait-slavering father. I don't want my name to be dragged down to *that* level. Goodbye.' *Click.*

James curled his fingers around his phone so tightly he was sure the screen would crack or his fingers. Possibly both. He swung his gaze to Aiesha's smile. Not a cat-got-the-canary one. A cat-got-the-whole-contents-of-the-aviary smile. A red mist of anger blurred his vision. He had to blink a couple of times to clear it. 'You little game-playing bitch,' he bit out. 'What the hell do you think you're doing?'

She pushed her lips out in a pout. 'That's hardly the way to address your brand-new mistress, is it?'

He clenched his jaw so firmly it reverberated inside his skull like a slammed door. 'No one will believe it. Not for a New York second.' Mental gulp. *I hope.*

Aiesha held up her phone again, scrolling through the feed of tweets, and began reading aloud. '"WTG! About time. Always knew JC had a thing for you."' She looked up at him with that bad girl smile of hers. 'Guess how many retweets so far?'

James swung away, ploughing a hand through his hair. How would he ever live this down? Everyone in London—*everyone on the planet*—would be rolling about the floor laughing at his choice of partner. A sluttish club singer who was sleeping her way up the social ladder like a poisonous viper winding its way up a vine.

Everyone would be saying it, the words he dreaded the most: like father, like son.

But wait...

Maybe there was a way he could switch this around. It would reflect badly on him if their 'relationship' was viewed as nothing more than a casual fling or temporary hook-up. He would look exactly like his father if he didn't go into damage control and fast.

Think. Think. Think.

Aha!

What if his relationship with Aiesha was a little more serious?

James took out his phone again and typed a quick tweet and pressed send before he was tempted to think twice. This could work. It had to work. Please God, let it work.

'What are you doing?' she asked. 'You can't retract it now. It's too late. It's gone viral.'

'I'm not retracting it.' He gave her a payback smile as he slipped his phone back in his pocket. 'Congratulations, Aiesha. You just got yourself engaged.'

CHAPTER THREE

Engaged?

Aiesha hid her surprise at his countermove behind her trademark screen of streetwise brashness. 'Do I get a big, flashy diamond ring with that?'

His smile dropped away and his deep blue eyes glittered with disgust as they took in the impudent height of her chin. 'You're the last person on earth I would ever consider becoming engaged to and you damn well know it. You're the one who set this up. Now you can deal with the consequences. We'll stay engaged until the press loses interest. I give it a couple of weeks, tops.'

Aiesha folded her arms across her chest, the action pushing her breasts up so that a generous hint of her cleavage showed. She enjoyed watching him try to keep his gaze north of her neckline. He was so starchy and uptight, but she knew that inside those crisply ironed trousers with their knife-sharp creases was a hot-blooded man in his prime. 'How much are you going to pay me for this little pretend gig? You should know by now I'm not the kind of girl to do anything for free…

even for…erm…' she gave him a little wink as she put her fingers up in mock quotation marks '"…family."'

His savage frown brought his brows together over his eyes. 'Have you no shame?'

She laughed at his schoolmasterish-stern expression because she knew it would annoy him. She *liked* annoying him. He was always so serious and sober. So grave and so disciplined. It amused her to niggle him, to watch him fight to control his temper. She watched as a dull flush rode high on his sharp aristocratic cheekbones and a muscle flickered in his jaw, on and off, as if it was being tugged by a surgical needle and thread beneath the skin.

Yep. He was furious with her all right. He looked as if he wanted to shake her until her teeth fell out and rolled along the floor like marbles.

But there was something else throbbing in the air and it wasn't anger.

Aiesha could feel the echo of it pulsing in her own body. She became aware of every one of her erogenous zones as if his steely gaze had burned through the ice that kept each of them in a deep-freeze lockdown.

Molten heat pooled between her thighs as she thought of those clenched hands relaxing enough to reach out and stroke her flesh, for one of those broad, masculine fingertips to brush across the pebble of each of her nipples, to tease the puckered skin until she gasped out loud with the pleasure.

She glanced at his tight-lipped mouth. She had always wondered how it would feel to have that mouth lose its rigidly disapproving lines and soften in passion, to meld to hers in a fiery lock of lust and longing, for his tongue to stab through the seam of her mouth to plunder hers.

Aiesha suppressed an involuntary shiver. She wasn't interested in being overcome with passion. Unlike most women, she could *always* separate sex from emotion. She could get down and dirty, but her heart and her head were never in it, only her body. Her body had needs and she saw to them if and when the right opportunity came along.

But something warned her about getting physical with James Challender, like a foghorn sounding in the distance. She couldn't put her finger on it, or describe it accurately, but she knew if she stepped over the boundary of becoming involved with him sexually then it might not just be her body that would receive him.

No one but no one had access to her heart and she was going to keep it that way.

His slate-blue eyes seared hers. 'How long have you been in contact with my mother?'

Aiesha held his accusing look with a defiant hoist of her chin. 'She wrote to me the year after her divorce from your father was finalised.'

His brows snapped together. 'You've been in contact *that* long?'

'On and off.'

'But…but why?'

Aiesha had been surprised by Louise's first phone call eight years ago. With the benefit of hindsight and a little more maturity, she knew she had acted appallingly to the only person who had ever shown her a shred of genuine affection.

Louise Challender had always wanted a daughter; she was the type of woman who should have had a brood of children to love and nurture, and yet she'd been unable to have another child after giving birth to James. It had put an enormous strain on her marriage to Clifford, but then Clifford wasn't the type of man who would have been a suitable father for anyone, let alone a brood of kids. He was too immature and selfish, like a spoilt child who had been overindulged and always expected everything to go his way. Aiesha had seen that from the moment she had been introduced to him when Louise brought her home from the streets, where she'd been living since her stepfather had kicked her out a week after her mother had overdosed on heroin. She'd refused to take her mother's place in his bed so he'd turned her out of the house, but not before committing an unspeakable act of cruelty that still caused her nightmares all these years on. If only she had thought to get Archie out of the house first.

If only. If only. If only...

Watching as her beloved dog was strangled to death in front of her had destroyed her belief in humanity. Archie had only yelped the once but his cry had haunted many a sleepless night since.

Aiesha blinked the distressing scene out of her head as best she could. She wasn't that powerless young girl any more. She was the one in control now. She allowed no man to have an advantage on her.

Clifford Challender might wear bespoke clothes and

speak with an upper-class accent but underneath he was no different from her brutish, despicable, drug-dealing stepfather. She had proven it. It had only taken five minutes alone with him in the study to set it up. She had planned it to the last detail. They'd agreed to meet at a hotel in London's West End to 'begin' their affair. Clifford had taken the bait—as she had known he would—with the press waiting to capture the moment, but, looking back now, she regretted that Louise had been hurt in the process.

Although she had never told Louise, or indeed anyone, how deeply traumatised she had been from that last interaction with her stepfather, over time she had been able to understand why she had behaved as she had. She had been so angry, so viciously angry, at the injustice dished out to her and to poor little Archie that she had come into the Challender household with the sole agenda to cause as much mayhem as she could. Like a wounded animal, she had scratched and bitten at the hand that was trying its best to comfort and feed her.

Aiesha had apologised to Louise since and they had never mentioned it again by tacit agreement. But if Louise was bitter or still held any resentment she certainly gave no sign of it. If anything, Aiesha got the impression that Louise was much happier without the shackles of a marriage that had limped along for years for the sake of appearances.

But James's bitterness was another thing entirely.

He hadn't forgiven her for the attention she had drawn to his family. Drunk on the power of payback, Aiesha had sold her story to the press. Although no crime had been committed, for Clifford Challender hadn't done anything other than agree to meet her, the press had run with the Lolita angle and run wild. Selling her story hadn't necessarily been about the money—although it had come in very handy at getting her set up until she came of age—but about showing the world she would not be ignored or silenced just because she was from the wrong side of the tracks.

The impact on the Challender name in the architectural sector had been catastrophic. At the time she hadn't thought or cared how her actions would impact on James, but impact they did. Along with his father, he'd lost current and potential clients, and it had only been in the last year or so that he had been able to redress the effects of the fallout of the scandal.

No wonder he hated her.

And no wonder he couldn't understand what possible reason his mother would have for staying in contact with her, even sporadically, much less invite her to stay in her home for as long as she wanted.

Aiesha wasn't sure she understood it herself.

'Your mother isn't one to bear grudges,' she said. 'Unlike someone else I know, she's prepared to let bygones be bygones.'

His glittering eyes, his knitted brow, his flared nostrils and his iron-hard jaw visibly quaked with contempt. 'My mother's a fool to be taken in by you again. You haven't changed an iota. You're still a smart-mouthed, conniving little gold-digging tramp on the make. The fact that you want money to pose as my fiancée proves it.'

Aiesha tossed her head in a devil-may-care manner. 'Take it or leave it, James. It's your reputation on the line, not mine. I don't have anything to lose.'

His hands balled into fists as if he didn't trust himself not to reach for her and do her an injury. A perverse part of her was excited to see him teetering on the cliff edge of the iron-strong self-control he so prided himself on possessing. It made her want to push and push and push until he fell into sin. It was why she goaded him so shamelessly. She wanted to prove he was no different from all the other men she'd had dealings with throughout her life. He might have been surrounded by silver spoons and salvers, and slept on silk and satin sheets, but behind that stiff, upper-lip, straitlaced demeanour was a brooding, simmering passion that was as primal and earthy as any other sexually mature man.

His eyes nailed hers like blue darts, his mouth so tightly set it looked physically as well as morally painful for him to get the words out. 'How much?'

Aiesha pictured the cottage in the country she had dreamed of since she was a little girl living in council flats with walls as thin as diet wafers. She had dreamed of a place surrounded by flowers and fields and forest, of peace and calm instead of shouting and swearing and fighting. No pimps. No drugs. No violence.

Solitude. *Safety.*

She named a figure that sent James's brows shooting towards his hairline. '*What?*' he choked.

She folded her arms in an implacable manner. 'You heard.'

He frowned at her blackly. 'You're joking, surely?'

'Nope.'

He coughed out a disbelieving laugh. 'This is ludicrous.' His hand scored a jagged pathway through his hair. 'Am I even having this conversation?'

'Want me to pinch you?'

He quickly stepped back from her, holding his hands up in front of himself like a barrier. 'Don't touch me.'

Aiesha smiled as she deliberately stepped closer. It was thrilling to have so much sensual power at her disposal. The air vibrated with electric voltage; she could feel it lifting the skin of her arms in a carpet of goose bumps and wondered if his body was undergoing the same sensual overload. Was his blood thundering through his veins, thickening him? Extending him to full erection? Was he feeling that primal ache that consumed everything but the desperate need to copulate?

Maybe she should ignore that silly little foghorn inside her head. What would it hurt to have a little bit of fun to pass the time? He had always been the subject of her fantasies.

Now she could make them real.

She lazily stroked her fingertip over the thick and neatly aligned Windsor knot of his tie, close to where a pulse was beating like a piston in his tanned and cologne-scented neck. She breathed in lemon and lime and something else that was elusive and yet potently addictive. 'What are you afraid of, posh boy?' Her fingers slipped down from the knot to play with the end of his tie like a mean cat with a mouse's tail. 'That this time around I might prove to be irresistible?'

She heard his jaw lock. Heard his teeth grind. Saw

his pupils flare as his eyes flicked to her mouth for a nanosecond.

'I can resist you.' His voice was so deep and so husky it sounded as if it had been scraped along a rough surface and only just survived the journey.

Aiesha looked at the dark pinpricks of regrowth surrounding his mouth and chin. He had a strong, uncompromising mouth, his top lip neatly sculpted, but his lower lip was fuller, rich with sensual promise. Something unfurled deep and low inside her belly, like a satin ribbon running away from its spool.

Suddenly the game she'd been playing turned deadly serious.

The battle of wills she was so sure she could win shifted its power balance. She felt it in the immeasurable beat of time where his gaze grazed her mouth again. It provoked a visceral reaction inside her body, a lightning strike of lust that all but knocked her off her feet.

She sent her tongue out over her lips to try and quell the fizzing sensation that was fast becoming an ache. His warm, faintly mint-scented breath skated over the surface of her lips as, centimetre by centimetre, millimetre by millimetre he ever so slowly began to close the distance. Her own breath felt painfully restricted as she drew it into her lungs, as if the space inside her chest was already taken up by something big and suffocating. She rose up on tiptoe, closing her eyes, waiting, waiting, waiting for that first blissful moment of contact...

Her eyes sprang open when she heard him take a step back from her. His expression was as stiff and formal as the wallpaper on the wall behind him. 'I'll deposit the money in your bank account once I have a legal contract drawn up,' he said.

She arched a brow. 'The terms being?'

'If you speak out of turn to the press you'll have to repay the amount in full plus twenty per cent interest.'

Aiesha pushed her pursed lips from side to side. 'Twenty per cent seems a bit steep to me. Let's make it ten.'

'Fifteen.'

'Five, or I tell the press right here and now we're having a tawdry little affair that will be over once this snow melts.'

His jaw worked for a moment before he gave a curt nod of agreement. But she wasn't sure if he was agreeing because he thought the deal fair or because he couldn't wait to get away from her. His brusque statement suggested the latter. 'I'm going to the study to work for the rest of the evening.'

Aiesha hitched one hip higher than the other in her best femme-fatale pose. 'All work and no play makes James a very dull boy.'

His eyes held hers in a tight little lock that made the backs of her knees tingle. 'I know how to play. I'm just a little more careful than most over choosing my playmates.'

She curved her mouth in a mocking manner. He might find it easy to resist her now but she wasn't finished with him yet. She would bring him to his knees before the week was out. He would not be so straitlaced and sure of himself once she had him where she wanted him. She could hardly wait.

'I bet Phoebe Frozen-Face doesn't do it up against the kitchen bench or outside under the stars on a hot sweaty night. I bet she's a bed and missionary girl with all the lights off. Am I right?'

His lips came together in a flat white line. 'Please spare me the sordid details of your sexual practices. I'm not interested.'

'Yes, you are.' Aiesha all but purred the words at him. 'I bet you're wondering what it would feel like to do me right here and now. On the rug at our feet. So rough one or both of us gets carpet burn.'

The words were provocative, goading, tempting. The erotic images they triggered in her mind even more so. She knew she was being utterly brazen but something about his steely resistance fired her determination to have him finally admit his desire for her. It was the ultimate challenge.

He was the ultimate challenge.

James gave her a dismissive look but she noticed the hammer was back in the lower quadrant of his jaw. 'Keep your Vegas-showgirl tactics for someone who actually gives a damn,' he said. 'I have far better things to do with my time.'

Aiesha watched as he turned and strode purposefully out of the room, his back and shoulders as stiff as a plank, his hands balled into fists as hard as cannonballs at his sides.

An anticipatory smile turned up the corners of her mouth.

I am so going to win this.

CHAPTER FOUR

JAMES STARED AT his computer screen, but instead of seeing the designs he'd drawn up for the Sherwood townhouse he saw Aiesha lying naked on the Persian rug in the sitting room with him pounding into her. Her hair was fanned out over the rug, her beautiful breasts jiggling sexily, her feline back arching as she came with a primal scream that—

He gave himself a mental slap and refocused on the project in front of him. The plans, which had seemed so brilliant the day before, now looked like a boring set of angles and planes.

He pushed himself back from the desk and stood and stretched the stiffness out of his back. That wasn't all that was stiff…but the less he thought about that the better.

He stood in front of the window, staring at the moonlit white-out outside. His Highland sanctuary had become a prison of torturous temptation. A temple of sinful longings. He was trapped inside a house with a wanton woman with seduction on her mind. Aiesha was on a mission and he was her target. How was he going to resist her? She was a potent cocktail of sass and sensuality. He was already drunk on looking at her. On smelling her exotic fragrance that seemed to be in every room of the house, following him, haunting him, tempting him. He was mesmerised by those unique eyes, transfixed by that sinfully luscious mouth and that lithe body with its catwalk sway of hips and pelvis. His body throbbed with such raw longing he considered plunging himself in the snow outside to cool off.

Everything about her turned him on. Her wilfulness, her naughty pouts, the way she tossed her hair over her shoulders like a flighty filly tossed its mane. The way her grey eyes looked at him knowingly, smoulderingly, with that come-and-get-me-I-know-you-want-to steadiness as if she could sense his lust for her lurking, thickening him beneath his clothes.

James muttered an expletive and turned away from the window. It was well past midnight and he hadn't eaten. He would kill for a glass of red wine but bringing alcohol into a situation like this was asking for the sort of trouble he could do without right now. Falling into Aiesha's honey trap was exactly what she expected him to do. It was what every man she set her sights on did. She collected men like trophies, the richer and more powerful the better. He was just another prize to tick off her list. One she had wanted a long time. It was her unfinished business—the seduction of the son and heir to complete her set—the father and now the son. He would be discarded like yesterday's news as soon as she proved what she wanted to prove.

James could only hope the fervid interest in their

relationship would die away once some other couple was targeted. He loathed being besieged by the press. It brought back the cringeworthy memories of the days after Aiesha had sold her story. The cameras had been set up outside his parents' London home for over a week. He hadn't been living at home at the time but that didn't stop the barrage of attention. He was set upon at his apartment in Notting Hill. Every day microphones were thrust in his face as he left for work, asking him for comments on his father's behaviour. They followed him everywhere, even during work hours. The intrusion was so bad at one point that one of his most important clients had taken his business to a rival firm.

It had taken him this long to build up trust with a good clientele and now Aiesha was back and up to her usual mischief.

James took Bonnie out for a last pit stop before doing the rounds of turning off the lights downstairs. He came to the sitting room, where the door was slightly ajar, the muted light of the side-table lamps creating a soft V-shaped beam across the floor of the hall.

He pushed the door open to find the coffee table in front of the sofa littered with the remains of a snatch-and-grab meal: an empty wine glass, a side plate with cheese fragments and a browned apple core on it, a scrunched-up paper napkin, an empty yogurt container and a sticky teaspoon, a trail of crumbs. *Typical.* She was swanning about the place like the lady of the manor, expecting everyone else to pick up after her. He wasn't running a hotel, for God's sake. Who did she think she was, leaving his mother's sitting room in such a state?

His gaze went to the sofa and found…Sleeping Beauty.

That was exactly what Aiesha looked like. She was lying on her side facing the fire that had burned down low in the grate, her cheek resting on one of the velvet scatter cushions, her arms tucked in close to her chest and her slim legs curled up like a child's. Her hair was tousled and loose about her shoulders, one curly tendril lying like an *S* on her cheek. In sleep she looked innocent and vulnerable, far younger than twenty-five.

The eight years difference in their ages suddenly felt like a century. Make that an entire geological period.

Should he wake her?

No!

James looked at the fire. It would make too much noise getting that going again. The room, along with the rest of the house, was centrally heated but set on a timer. He could feel the slight chill in the air as the ormolu clock on the mantelpiece ticked its way to 1:00 a.m.

His gaze went to the mohair throw rug draped over the back of the wing chair. Should he or shouldn't he? He debated with himself for another thirty seconds as he watched her sleep. Her chest rose and fell, her soft mouth opening slightly as her breath came out on a sigh. Her eyelids with their spider-leg-long lashes fluttered and her forehead puckered as if something she was dreaming about had disturbed her. But after a moment or two her forehead smoothed out and she burrowed deeper into the sofa cushions like a dormouse curling up for winter.

James waited another half a minute before stealthily tiptoeing across the carpet like a burglar to get the throw rug—mentally rolling his eyes at the ridiculousness of his caution—and brought it back to gently cover her with it.

It was as if he had dropped a plank of timber on her.

She suddenly leapt off the sofa and struck out with her fists, catching him on the side of the nose in a glancing blow that made stars explode behind his eyes.

James swore and, stumbling backwards, cupped his hand over his throbbing nose, the blood dripping through his fingers to the carpet at his feet. Pain pulsed in sickening waves through his face, his skull and his stomach. He swayed on his feet as he fought against the dizziness as a school of silverfish floated before his gaze.

Aiesha reeled back from him, speaking through her hands that were clasped over her mouth in stunned horror. 'Oh, my God! Did I hurt you?'

'No,' he said through clenched teeth as he reached with his other hand for his handkerchief to stem the flow of blood. 'I have spontaneous nosebleeds all the time.'

Her eyes were still as wide as her discarded dinner plate. 'I'm sorry. I—I didn't know who it was.'

He glared at her over the wad of his handkerchief. His nose was still pulsating with eye-watering pain as it hosed blood. What was she thinking, swinging at him like that? *She* was the intruder, not him. 'Who the hell did you *think* it was?'

Her teeth chewed at her lower lip, her gaze falling away from his as she backed out of the room. 'Erm… I'll go and get you some ice…'

* * *

Aiesha held a hand against her juddering heart as she stumbled to the kitchen. The shock of waking to see a dark shape looming over her had made her react on instinct. Her primal brain hadn't had time to recognise it was not some predatory lecher after a quick feel. Her instinctive reaction to hit out was something she'd learned from a young age, having to dodge the inappropriate attention from her mother's collection of unsavoury partners. It was why she never spent the whole night with anyone. Ever. It was too awkward explaining her restlessness…or the nightmares. The last time she'd had a nightmare she'd wet the bed.

Try explaining *that* to a lover.

Aiesha looked at her reddened knuckles. If the pain throbbing in them was any indication, James was going to have a shiner by morning, if not sooner.

Her heart was not quite back where it belonged when she came back with a therapeutic ice pack she'd found in the freezer.

James was sitting on the sofa she had fallen asleep on earlier, his head tilted back, the strong column of his throat exposed. He opened one eye to look at her. 'That's a mean right hook you've got there.'

Aiesha averted her gaze as she handed him the ice pack. 'I took up boxing classes a couple of years ago. It's great for fitness. You should try it.'

He winced as he pressed the pack to the bridge of his nose. 'Somehow, the thought of thumping an opponent until they lose consciousness doesn't appeal.'

She bit her lip again. 'Does it hurt terribly?'

He gave her a look. 'That was the intention, wasn't it?'

Aiesha walked over to the remains of the fire and gave it a futile poke. She could sense his watchful gaze resting on her. He'd found her asleep. Off guard. Vulnerable. Had she given anything away while sleeping? Murmured anything? Revealed anything of the turmoil of her past?

She tamed her body language the way she'd been doing since she was eight years old. *Show no emotion. Show no fear.* 'I don't like people sneaking up on me.'

'I was trying to make you comfortable. You were lying asleep in front of a dead fire. I was worried you might be cold.'

Worried? Ha. When had anyone been concerned about her welfare? She was invisible unless she *made* people notice her. She had spent her life as an outsider. Not good enough. Not educated enough. Not posh enough.

The thought of him caring about her comfort disturbed her. No one cared about her. No one watched out for her. Not unless they wanted something.

Aiesha turned and squared her gaze with his. 'Why didn't you wake me up? Why creep around and scare the crap out of me? I'm glad I punched you. I should've hit you harder.'

He took the ice pack away from his face, frowning at her, but not in anger. There was something measuring about his gaze as it held hers. She looked away, flattening her mouth, locking him out.

He came over to where she was standing in front of the dead fire. 'You want to hit me again?' he asked.

'Come on. Put up your fists and clobber me with your best shot.'

She crossed her arms, flashing him a cutting glare. 'Stop making fun of me.'

Those dark blue eyes continued to penetrate and probe. 'I'm not joking, Aiesha. Get it out of your system. You want to hit me, then go ahead and hit me. I won't hit you back. I can take it like a man.'

Aiesha clenched her fists. She *could* hit him. She could probably knock him out cold if she put her mind to it. Trouble was, her mind was out of sync with her heart.

She hated that she'd hurt him. She loathed violence. Violence sickened her. She'd only taken up boxing as a precaution while living in Vegas. It wasn't called Sin City for nothing. Men with too much alcohol on board thought it their right to grope and proposition her each night as she left the club. She had never hit anyone before, just a punching bag in the gym. That punching bag had been the substitute for all the men she wished she'd been able to pummel back the way they had pummelled her mother. Hadn't she herself copped enough hits and slaps in her time to want to eradicate all violence from the world?

And then there was poor little Archie. He had trusted her to keep him safe from that despicable Beast Man and she had failed him. She tried to block the sound of that startled yelp inside her brain. She tried to block the sound of that fatal crack, as poor little Archie's neck was broken. She tried to block the sight of that poor little limp body hanging from Beast Man's horrible hand like a trophy.

Aiesha could feel her defences crumbling like the ashes of the log she'd poked in the grate a minute ago. James had seen her off guard. Unprotected by her outer shell of hard-nosed tart. Her fight-or-flight instincts were battling it out inside her chest. She could feel every moment of the struggle like fists landing heavy blows against her heart.

Flee.

Fight.

Flee.

Fight.

She was conscious of the silence…measured by the sound of the ticking clock on the mantelpiece above the fireplace. She was conscious of the dryness of her mouth and the unfamiliar hot moist prickling at the back of her eyes. She was conscious of a tight restriction as the deep well of her buried emotion bubbled up in her throat like a foul sewer.

She. Would. Not. Cry.

Aiesha blinked and quickly slipped her armour back on. She opened and closed her hands, testing him. Watching to see if he so much as flinched. 'I could really hurt you,' she said.

'Undoubtedly.'

She couldn't make out his expression. Was he testing her? Seeing if she would take up the dare? She brought her hand up but he didn't move a muscle. His gaze was steady on hers. She placed her hand on the side of his face, her skin catching on the graze of his stubble.

Something caught in her chest. A snag. A hitch. Then a letting go...

There was another heartbeat of silence.

He covered her hand with his, holding it within the gentle prison of his fingers. 'That the best you could do?' he said.

Aiesha looked at his mouth before flicking her gaze back to his. 'I don't want to ruin that pretty-boy face of yours.'

The dark blue of his eyes intensified, holding hers in a lock that made something inside her belly tilt and then spill. 'You're scared.'

She sent her tongue out in a quick darting movement to moisten her lips. 'Let me go, James.'

'I have a little forfeit to collect first.'

Something dropped off a shelf in her stomach. 'Forfeit?'

He spread his hands through the mane of her hair, his gaze moving from her eyes to her mouth in a slow and mesmerising fashion. 'You punched me in the nose. I get to kiss you. Fair's fair.'

She affected a sneer but was pretty sure it was wide off the mark. 'Is that meant to be a punishment?'

'Why don't we find out?' he said and, tugging her against him, his mouth came down over hers.

His lips were warm and firm, slow and deliberate. Purposeful. His tongue stroked against her top lip and then her lower lip without deepening the kiss. It sent every one of Aiesha's nerves into a frenzied clamour of want. She wound her arms around his neck, leaning into him to give more of herself to the kiss. She opened her mouth, inviting him in, teasing him with the flicker of her tongue against his lips.

He made a deep growling sound in the back of his throat and thrust his tongue against hers, wrangling and tangling with it, sending her pulses soaring. He tasted unique, not sour or beery, or stale or too mouth-washy or minty.

He tasted...*just right.*

Aiesha delved her fingers into his thick dark hair as he continued to explore her mouth in spine-loosening detail. Her body trembled with desire, great giant waves of it coursing through her as his tongue moved inside her mouth with erotic intent. His kiss was mesmerising, magical and intoxicating. Not rushed and greedy, but respectful and enticing. Her mouth responded to him like a flower opening to warm rays of sunshine. She had been kissed too many times to count but not one of them had been like this. Gentle and yet determined, passionate and yet controlled.

His pelvis was pressed against hers, his erection leaving her in no doubt of the effect she was having on him. She could feel the length of it against her belly, making her desperate to touch him skin on skin. She felt her inner core contract, the silky moisture of arousal anointing her in anticipation of his possession.

His breathing was heavy, as if he was only just hold-ing on to his self-control. She felt the tension in him, the way his hands were holding her by the hips, set there, anchored there as if moving them to another part of her body would be dangerous.

She made a mewling sound as his teeth grazed her

lower lip, tugging on it before salving it with the stroke of his tongue. He repeated the process with her top lip, little teasing nips and tugs that made the hairs on the back of her neck quiver. He smoothly glided his tongue back into her mouth, sweeping hers up into a tango of lustful longings.

Aiesha wanted him so badly she could feel it writhing and coiling like a serpent inside her. Had she ever wanted a man more than James Challender? He was the ultimate prize. Rich, powerful, well-to-do. She had *always* wanted him. From the first moment she had met him when he came to visit his parents soon after she had come to stay she had felt a lightning flash of awareness arc between them. He had kept a respectful distance, making it abundantly clear he was not going to be seduced by a teenager. He hadn't been rude to her or cruel. He had been polite but firm. Implacable. And back then she had hated him for it.

Now…now she wasn't quite so sure what she felt other than rip-roaring lust.

She wanted him because he represented everything she had missed out on during her harrowing childhood. Success. Stability. Safety.

She made a move for his belt buckle but he stalled her hand, holding it against him as he fought to control his breathing.

'No,' he said.

No?

What man had ever said no to her? Ever since she was a kid she'd been fighting them off. Rejecting *them*, not them rejecting her. The shift in power was new and troubling…unsettling. She liked to be the one who said yay or nay. 'You want me.' She said it matter-of-factly. Without emotion.

He released her hand and stepped back from her. 'This can't go anywhere.' He pushed his hair back over his forehead. 'You know it can't.'

Aiesha hid behind her mask of brash bad girl. 'Too rough for your upmarket taste?'

His frown carved deeply into his brow as he moved away to the door to leave. 'I think it's best if we keep things on a platonic basis. It's…safer that way.'

She cocked one of her eyebrows at him in a cheeky manner. 'So we're friends now instead of enemies?'

He turned and looked back at her for a long moment. 'I suspect your only enemy, Aiesha, is yourself.' He punctuated his comment with a brisk dismissive nod and closed the door before she could think of a comeback.

CHAPTER FIVE

JAMES CLOSED HIS bedroom door with a self-recriminating curse. *Are you crazy? Kissing her? Touching her? Wanting her?* He pushed a hand through his hair in distraction. He should *never* have kissed her. He'd crossed the line. The line he'd put down a decade ago.

Aiesha was cunning and clever. For a moment there he'd sensed a softening in her. Her guard had slipped, or so he'd thought. But she knew exactly what she was doing. Which buttons of his to press. She wasn't the emotionally vulnerable type. She was too hard-boiled, too street smart. Hadn't her punch proved that?

He grimaced as he checked his reflection in the mirror of his en-suite bathroom. His nose wasn't broken but he was going to have a black eye for sure, all because he had come too close to her without her knowing.

He rubbed at the stubble on his jaw. She'd been soundly asleep; there was no way he had got that wrong. Her breathing had been deep and even, her whole body relaxed. Her reaction had been so extreme, so unexpected. *Why?*

He thought about her background…trying to recall

what his mother had told him about her in the past. Aiesha had been vague about her family of origin; the only thing she'd told his mother was that she was a teenage runaway and it had been her choice to leave. She hadn't been with his family long enough to prise out any other details. As far as he knew, she hadn't been into drugs or heavily into alcohol, or at least not that he had noticed. She only had one tattoo, and a small one at that, on the underside of her right wrist—the name Archie with hearts and roses—but she had never said who Archie was or why he was so important to her that she'd felt compelled to have his name permanently inked into her skin.

James cursed again. Kissing her had been a mistake. A big mistake. A ginormous mistake. He'd known it but done it anyway. He hadn't been able to stop himself. As soon as she had put her hand so gently on his face he'd known he was going to kiss her. It had been inevitable. A force outside his control. He'd only planned to press his mouth to hers as an experiment, as a test for himself. To prove he could do it without losing his head.

For years he had dreamed of kissing that mouth. He had fantasised about it. Hungered for it like a former addict did a forbidden drug. Her mouth was as addictive as he'd imagined it—soft and sweet and yet hot and hungry. The blood had surged through him at rocket-force speed. Her deliciously feminine body had felt so...*so right* as he'd held her in his arms. The way her mouth had tasted, the way her tongue had danced with his in that sexy tango, the way her hips had been in the perfect position against his. He'd wanted her so badly he'd had to fight to keep his hands in one place so he didn't use them to tear the clothes from her body and ram himself into her wickedly tempting wetness.

He was not a man who acted on impulse. He did not indulge in casual affairs or shallow hook-ups. He had needs and he saw to them in a responsible and respect-ful manner. His life was carefully planned and detailed, organised and compartmentalised because that was the way to avoid nasty surprises. He had seen too many friends and colleagues—not to mention his father—come unstuck by succumbing to a reckless ill-timed roll in the sack. Careers, reputations, familial relation-ships were permanently ruined in the carnage of an il-licit affair and he would not make the same mistake.

His father's double life had come to light during James's late teens. Throughout his childhood, when-ever he was home from boarding school, his mother would do her happy-families thing and James had never questioned it. Hadn't thought to question it. Maybe he hadn't wanted to face it. On some level he'd known his parents weren't blissfully honeymoon-like happy, but neither had he thought they were utterly miserable. They were his parents and he liked that they were to-gether and seemingly stable. But then, when he'd been in his final year, someone at school had made a com-ment about seeing James's father coming out of a hotel with a woman in the city and James's concept of a sta-ble home life had been shattered. His mother had sto-ically tried to keep the marriage together for the next few years after his father promised to remain faithful, but of course Clifford had strayed time and time again, albeit a little more discreetly.

Ever since, James swore he would not live like his father, lying and cheating his way through life. He would not be swayed by temptation or sabotage his success and reputation by a lack of self-control.

But there were two things he couldn't control in his life right now—Aiesha Adams and the weather. He pulled back the curtains and looked at the flakes of snow falling past his window.

Fabulous.

Freaking fabulous.

Aiesha waited until James had left the house before she came downstairs the next morning. She saw him talking on his mobile as he headed to the river walk with Bonnie. He had his head down and his shoulders hunched forwards against the wind. He stopped a couple of times to glance back frowningly at the house but Aiesha kept out of sight behind the edge of the curtain. Even from this distance she could see the colourful bruise beneath his eye. Was he still wondering why she had gone at him like that?

She gave a long sigh when he disappeared into the fringe of trees along the river. Why should she care what he thought of her? What was the point of trying to whitewash her reputation now? He would never see her as anything other than a good-time bad girl.

She had to shake off this restless mood...and there was only one way to do it.

The ballroom was her favourite room at Lochbannon. It was next to the sitting room and overlooked the formal gardens at the front of the house. Watermarked silk curtains hung in large swathes at the windows, the bottoms lying in billowing pools on the highly polished parquet floor like the trains of elegant ball gowns. A central chandelier dripping with sparkling crystals hung from the ceiling and various velvet-shaded wall lights added to the sense of grandeur. The piano was a concert grand and had been recently tuned. Louise had always insisted the piano was regularly serviced but Aiesha had a sneaking suspicion Louise had quickly organised it once she had known Aiesha was coming to stay.

Louise was an accomplished violinist but had given up her musical aspirations to marry Clifford Challender. He had insisted on being the only star on the Challender family stage. Louise was required to be the supporting act, to grace his table with her congenial presence, to turn a blind eye to any extracurricular activities he indulged in from time to time, and to bring up his son according to the rules of the upper class.

It reminded Aiesha of her mother's fitting-in-with-men mentality. It had started with Aiesha's father, who had dominated her mother as soon as he got her pregnant. Her mother had done everything she was told to and yet was still punished for whatever he took offence to. It could be the way the housework was done or the way the meal was cooked, or the way she looked or didn't look. An opinion expressed that didn't tie in with the rules and regulations he set down. It had been impossible for her mother to gauge what was right or wrong. Her self-esteem had taken even more of a battering than her body.

And yet, after Aiesha's father had been locked away for armed robbery, instead of the new life Aiesha had envisaged, her mother had drifted into another relationship with the same old pattern developing within a matter of weeks. It happened repeatedly. Her mother would finally get the courage to leave and within weeks she would find someone else who was a carbon copy of the man she'd just escaped from. It was the drugs that did it. They were the lure each and every time. The mild addiction Aiesha's father had started with a joint had grown into an uncontrollable habit. Heroin, cocaine, alcohol—anything that offered a temporary respite from reality. Her mother had been charmed time and time again by manipulative men who promised her the world and gave her nothing but heartache, and finally death.

Aiesha looked at the walnut cabinet where row after row of musical scores were stored. All the classics were there as well as a selection of more modern pieces. She thought of Louise's talent, all those hours and hours of practice and personal sacrifice to make it to the top tier of musical performance, wasted on a man who hadn't appreciated her.

From the first moment Aiesha had stepped over the threshold of the Challender mansion in Mayfair she burned with envy over James's childhood. What she would have given for such luxury, for such comfort. For a full night's sleep without some sleazy beer-sodden creep sneaking up on her. For a roof over her head each

night, for regular meals, a top-notch education, and holi-
days to somewhere warm and exotic and exciting.

But now she wondered if he, too, had suffered from
neglect. Nothing like the neglect she had suffered, but
the type that left other sorts of scars.

Growing up with a selfish, limelight-stealing father
would be enormously difficult, if not at times downright
embarrassing. Trying to please someone who could
never be pleased. Trying to live down the shame of having his father's playboy behaviour splashed over every
paper while his mother suffered in silence at home.

The weeks after Aiesha's story broke were intense for
him and his mother. She had seen the footage of James
being chased along the street outside his Notting Hill
residence and again in front of the office block where
he had his architectural business. His father's peccadil-
loes had brought enormous shame to him then and now.

Was that why James was so much of a workaholic
and perfectionist? Driven and focused to the exclusion
of all else, in particular fun? Was that why he had those
lines of strain around his mouth and two horizontal ones
on his forehead? He frowned more than he smiled. He
worked rather than played. Was that why he had chosen
such a boring and predictable woman to marry? Phoebe
Trentonfield was probably a nice enough person, but she
wasn't right for him. He needed someone who would
stand up to him. To push him out of the nice little safe
comfort zone he had created for himself.

Someone who would release the locked down passion in him.

Someone like me...

Aiesha pulled out the shiny black piano stool and sat down heavily on the thought. She wasn't the type of girl a man like James would settle down with. She didn't tick any of his neat little boxes.

She was from the wrong side of town.

She was from the wrong side of everything.

Men like James Challender did not get involved with Vegas lounge singers who had a father in prison and a stepfather who should be.

Men like James chose girls who were polished and cultured, women who had a blue-blood pedigree centuries long. Aristocrats who knew which cutlery to use during which course and who never put a high-heeled, designer-clad foot wrong.

Aiesha put her hands over the keys, opening and closing them to warm them up. Her bruised knuckles protested at the movement but she ignored them. She was used to pain. She knew all its forms. Physical pain was the easiest to deal with.

Emotional pain was the one she had to avoid.

'Are you out of your mind?' Clifford Challender roared at James via his mobile while he was out walking Bonnie. 'That little slut will ruin your reputation and laugh in your face while she's doing it.'

James refrained from disclosing to his father the truth about his relationship with Aiesha. It wasn't just because of the punch and kiss and make-up incident last night, which he was still trying to wrap his head around. Clifford was not the discreet type. The news of his sham engagement would be all over social media come his father's first vodka of the day. Although, judging from the tone of his father's voice, he suspected he had already sunk a couple of shots and it wasn't even 10:00 a.m.

'I keep out of your affairs. Please keep out of mine.'

'I blame your mother for this,' Clifford said. 'She's always been a sucker for a lame duck. That girl will take her for another ride. Just shows what a stupid fool she is to fall for it a second time.'

James was glad his father was close to a thousand kilometres away, otherwise he might have been tempted to give him a black eye to match his own spectacular one. He hated the way his father used every opportunity to trash his mother since the divorce. It was his father's way of shifting the blame off himself. In Clifford's mind, James's mother had ruined everything by 'making a fuss' about his occasional affairs.

Although James was furious with Aiesha about her methods, he was privately relieved the scandal had brought on the divorce that should have happened years before. 'I've already warned you about speaking about Mum like that.'

'You don't think she set this up?' Clifford said.

'No.' *Yes. No. Maybe. I don't know.* He hadn't told his mother he was coming to Lochbannon. He hadn't even told her he was thinking of asking Phoebe to marry him. It was coincidence. Happenstance. *Wasn't it?* 'Mum had to leave the country at short notice. I haven't talked to her since she texted me.'

Clifford made a scornful sound. 'I don't give your engagement to that little bit of trailer trash a month. You haven't got the balls to handle a chit like that. Stick to your nice girls, son. Leave the bad ones to me.'

James put his phone away, and then stopped and looked back at the house in the distance. He was assailed by two very different thoughts. First, sticking to a nice girl suddenly seemed very unappealing and second, the thought of Aiesha being anywhere near his father suddenly sent a shudder running down his spine.

James was coming back from his bracing walk to the woods when he heard the music coming from the ballroom. It was like nothing he had heard from there before. And it wasn't anything he would hear in a Las Vegas lounge bar, either. It was lilting and melodic and yet…strangely haunting. The cadences were deeply poignant, touching on a chord deep inside him, like someone plucking on the strings of a hidden harp.

He stood at the door of the room, watching as Aiesha's hands danced over the keys of the piano. She was dressed in a hot-pink velour tracksuit that had teddy-bear ears on the hooded top, which she'd pulled over her head, presumably to keep her own ears warm. The look was quaint, cute and endearing. It showed a side of her that was young and playful, as if she didn't care what people thought of her attire as long as she was comfortable. She had a fierce frown of concentration on her forehead, although there was no musical score in front of her. She seemed totally unaware of anything but the music she was playing.

He was transfixed by the sound. Rising and falling notes that tugged and twitched on his heartstrings, minor key chords that were like emotional hits to his chest. Feelings he hadn't encountered for decades came out of hiding. They crowded his chest cavity until he could barely breathe, like too many guests at a cocktail party.

She came to the end of the piece and closed her eyes and bowed her head as if the effort had totally exhausted her.

James stepped into the room and she jolted upright like a puppet being jerked back up by its strings. 'You might've knocked,' she said with a frown of reproach.

'I didn't realise it was a private performance.'

She got up smartly from the piano and crossed her arms over her body in that keep-away-from-me gesture he was coming to know so well. A faint blush was on her cheeks, which she tried to hide by turning her back to look out of the window, where the sun was trying to get its act together but making a lacklustre job of it.

Her teddy-bear ears looked even cuter from behind.

So did her toosh.

'Nice walk?' she asked.

'Did you watch me leave?' Was that why she had chosen to play such beautifully evocative music while he was out of the house?

She didn't turn around. 'Pretty hard to ignore that dog's crazy yapping.'

'That dog has a name.'

This time she did turn around. Her expression showed nothing. Zip. 'Your eye looks terrible.'

James shrugged. 'Just as well there are no photographers lurking around.'

'The roads are still blocked?'

'Well and truly.'

She didn't show disappointment or relief. She showed nothing. Her face was a blank canvas. But two of her fingers fiddled with the zip on her tracksuit jacket, the sound of metal clicking against metal as rhythmic as a metronome.

He moved across the floor to the piano, tinkling a few keys to break the silence. 'What was that piece you were playing?'

'Why do you ask?'

He turned and caught the tail end of her guarded expression. 'I liked it. It was...' he searched for the right word '...stirring.'

She walked over to the walnut shelving where all of his mother's music was stored, her fingers playing along the spines like a child trailing a stick along a picket fence. James wondered if she was going to answer him. It seemed like for ever before she let her fingers fall away from the spines with a sigh he saw rather than heard. 'It's called *An Ode to Archie*.'

'You composed that yourself?'

'Yeah, what of it?' Her eyes flashed at him. 'You think just because I'm a club singer I can't write music or something?'

'Did you write it for the Archie on your wrist?'

Her left hand encircled her right wrist protectively, chin up, eyes still glittering. 'Yes.'

'Who is he?'

'Was.'

She moved away from the cabinet to go back to the

piano. She closed the lid over the keys like someone closing a conversation…or a coffin. A shiver scuttled over the back of James's neck like the legs of a spooked spider. 'He's dead,' she said.

'I'm sorry.'

She gave a shrug but he couldn't decide if it was a 'thank you' or 'I don't need your sympathy' one.

'Who was he?'

Her eyes met his but there was no sign of anything resembling emotion. A curtain was drawn. A shutter was down. 'He was a friend I had once. A childhood friend.'

'What happened to him?'

Her gaze moved away again. 'Do you play a musical instrument?'

The swift change of subject alerted him to an undercurrent of emotion she seemed at great pains to conceal. He was intrigued by her shadow self. The side he had seen last night when she had sprung up from that sofa with her fists at the ready. The side of her he briefly glimpsed while she sat playing her music. She was capable of deep feeling. No one who wrote music like that could possibly be cold and indifferent, without feeling and depth. But, rather than push her, he decided to leave it. For now.

'I'm afraid I didn't inherit my mother's musical ability. I'm sure it was a bitter disappointment to her. I think she would've liked me to be a virtuoso of some sort.'

She pushed the hood back off her cloud of tousled hair to face him levelly. 'Your father was wrong to make her give up her career.'

James studied her expression for a moment. 'She told you about that?'

She pressed her lips together as if regretting having spoken. 'I don't think she's disappointed you didn't pursue music as a career. She's very proud of your work, as any decent parent should be. You're good at what you do. Brilliant, actually. Everyone raves about your designs. They're so innovative.'

He gave her a wry look. 'A compliment from the cynical Aiesha Adams. Well, I'll be damned.'

'Make the most of it. It won't happen again.'

She moved past him to leave but he captured her arm on the way past. He hadn't consciously realised he was going to touch her until he felt his fingers wrap around her slim arm. Even through the soft velour of her tracksuit sleeve he could feel the snap-crackle-pop shock of his touch on her.

She glowered at him. 'If you want the other eye to match your right one then keep on doing what you're doing.'

'What am I doing?'

'You're touching me.'

He kept his gaze locked on her fiery one as his thumb found the thud of her pulse. 'I thought you liked being touched by me. I thought that was your plan. To seduce me.'

She pulled back from his hold but his fingers tightened. So did his groin. 'I've changed my mind.'

Her game plan had changed. She was back-pedalling after coming on so strong. He had got too close. Seen a part of her she didn't want to reveal. He had never met a more fascinating person. She was all smoke and mirrors. Secrets and cover-ups. It made him want her all the more. She was unpredictable. Mysterious. Captivating.

He moved in closer, breathing in the exotic gardenia-like flowery scent of her, watching as her black pupils in that stormy sea of grey grew wider. Her nostrils flared as if she, too, were breathing in his smell like a she wolf did a mate. Primal need overruled his common sense. His body blanked out the warnings of his mind like a master switch turning off a source of power, rerouting it to where it was needed the most. Blood flowed thick and strong to his groin. He felt it surging there in a hot turgid tide that no sandbag of rationality was ever going to withstand.

He hadn't realised it would be so hard to fight it. To deny it. To ignore it. His desire for her had smouldered in his blood and body for so long it took nothing but a look or touch to set it raging. 'You don't like it when someone else is in control, do you?' he said. 'You like to drum up the action but you don't like being on the receiving end of it. That's way too submissive for you, isn't it?'

She continued to glare at him but every now and again her gaze would flick down to his mouth as if remembering how it had felt to have it fused with her own. The tip of her tongue passed over her lips, leaving them moist and shimmering. She could have moved away if she wanted to. He had deliberately relaxed his hold; his fingers were barely more than a loose bracelet around her wrist.

He brought his head down and heard the sharp intake of her breath as his mouth came down to hover above hers. Their breaths mingled. Her pulse raced beneath his fingers. His skyrocketed. 'You know I want you,' he said.

'So?' Her voice lacked its usual sassy edge. It sounded thready. Uncertain. As if she had somehow drifted out of her depth and wasn't sure how to get back to safety. But even so her body swayed towards his like a fragment of metal being pulled by a magnet.

He brushed his bottom lip against her top one, a teasing nudge. A come-and-play-with-me invitation. 'So maybe it's time I did something about it.'

'Enter a monastery.'

He smiled against her lower lip. 'There's a thought.'

'If you kiss me you're a dead man.'

'So shoot me,' he said, and covered her mouth with his.

CHAPTER SIX

OF COURSE AIESHA didn't kill him. She didn't even pull away. She opened her mouth to the first hot commanding probe of his tongue and let the lust that smouldered between them run free. It was like the flare of a struck match following a trail of fuel. It licked along at breakneck speed, consuming everything along its way. It didn't matter that she wasn't in control any more. She needed this—*needed him*—like she needed air to breathe.

His mouth plundered hers, deeply, erotically, thoroughly. His tongue tangled with hers, playfully and then purposefully. Demanding hers to submit to his. She whimpered at his masterful command; he had taken control of her mouth and there was nothing she could do but respond. The thrill of his kiss made her body shiver with delight. Her senses went into a tailspin. Her heart jumped and leapt and sprinted. Her breathing became laboured as she tried to keep up with the madcap pace of his untrammelled passion.

His hands weren't content to hold her by the hips this time. This time they were everywhere. Her hair, the small of her back to press her close against his erection, then cupping her breasts, then tugging at her clothes as she tugged and pulled at his.

She gasped as his hand uncovered her breast. His hand was still cold from being outdoors, but it didn't matter as her body was sizzling hot. She was burning up with molten heat. She could feel it coursing through her body like a red-hot tide.

His thumb rolled over her nipple, back and forth, round and round, making her flesh pucker and tighten and every nerve wriggle and leap in rapture. So few men knew how to handle a woman's breast. He did. Not too hard. Not too soft. He seemed to read her body, gauging its needs like a maestro did a temperamental instrument. The strings of her desire buried deep in her body tightened, hummed and sang.

His mouth left hers to suckle on her breast, drawing her nipple deep into his mouth, his tongue rolling and circling, rolling and circling while her legs all but folded beneath her. He switched to her other breast, lavishing it with the same wickedly arousing attention.

He moved to the underside of her breast where the skin was supersensitive. No one had ever kissed her there before. No one had ever moved their lips on her with such careful and gentle attention. His lips moved over her skin like a fine sable brush moving over a priceless work of art.

He came back to her mouth, sweeping her away again on a hot, drugging kiss. That was why he was so bewitching. He could be so gentle and yet so passionate. Her body responded with deep clamouring longing, her insides squeezing and contracting with pleasure at the thought of him finally giving in to his desire for her. He was not trying to disguise it. He was not trying to deny it. He was giving it full rein and it was exactly like a bolting horse—fast, furious and unstoppable.

But she wasn't letting him have it all his own way. She got his belt out of his trouser lugs and unzipped him in a matter of seconds, taking the hot, hard, pulsing heat of him in her hands, stroking him, caressing every inch of his potent length until he was oozing with pre-ejaculatory fluid.

He gave an agonised groan. 'You're killing me.'

She sent him a sultry smile. 'Told you you're a dead man.'

He sucked in a harsh-sounding breath and pulled her hands away, holding them in a steely grip that made her insides contort with restless need at the latent strength he possessed. 'No. Wait. Not like this.'

Was he having second thoughts? Pulling away from her intellectually as well as physically? *Rejecting her?* Aiesha kept her tone light and teasing even though disappointment stalked her. 'You're not frightened of a little carpet burn, are you?'

His dark blue eyes searched hers for a moment. 'I want you so badly I'd lie on a bed of sizzling hot coals or nails. Or both.'

'But?' Her heart sank a little further. 'There's a but coming, isn't there?'

His fingers loosened around her wrists, his thumbs moving over the backs of her hands in a slow, stroking motion, his eyes still holding hers. 'I never have sex outside of a formal relationship.'

'No one-night stands?'

'No.'

Somehow it didn't surprise her. He would always colour between the lines. There was no hint of rebel in him. He was cautious by nature, sensible. He led rather than followed. He controlled rather than being swayed by impulse. He didn't have to look back on all the wrong choices he had made. He probably slept through each night without a single niggle of doubt or self-recrimination to disturb him.

'You don't know what you're missing,' she said. *Loneliness. Emptiness.* 'Think of the money you'd have saved on dates if you just got the deed done on the first night.'

He kept holding her hands. Kept holding her gaze in that studied way of his that made her feel he was seeing through the brash layers of bolshiness to the sensitive and wounded girl within. Aiesha would have squirmed but she was too well trained. Years spent hiding her feelings had made her a master at keeping the facade intact. She might have lapsed last night while he found her sleeping, but the front was up again and it was staying up.

'I like to get to know a person before I have sex with them,' he said.

Aiesha gave him a bold smile. 'Hi, I'm Aiesha. I'm twenty-five, almost twenty-six, and I'm a Vegas lounge singer. Well, I was until a few days ago. I'm currently unemployed.'

'How did you end up working in Vegas?'

She could feel her smile faltering and worked hard to keep it in shape. She wasn't going to tell him she had followed a dream only to have it blow away on the Nevada dust. The audition she had thought would be her big break had turned out to be for a job in a lingerie bar. Playing the piano in her underwear wasn't her thing, nor was doing erotic dance tricks on a stripper's pole to eke out tips from gawping men, but by then her money had been running too low to fly back to London. She had taken the lounge-singer job instead, hoping it would be a springboard to getting noticed as a serious musician. But she'd soon found out no one cared a jot who was behind the piano as long as it got played. 'I liked the party atmosphere. And the weather. It was a change from cold and wet and dismal London.'

He studied her for another long moment, his expression hard to read. 'Favourite colour?'

'It's a toss-up between pink and blue. I can never decide.'

The left side of his mouth kicked up half a centimetre. 'Best friend?'

Aiesha looked at him numbly. 'Um…pass.'

His half smile was quickly replaced with a frown. 'Are you saying you don't have a best friend?'

'I have friends.' *None that I trust.* 'I just don't have a best one.' Not any more.

'How do you like to spend your spare time?'

Aiesha made sure she didn't have spare time. Any breaks she took were packed with activity. Spare time allowed thoughts to creep in and ghosts from the past to haunt her. But then, relaxing wasn't something she had learned as a child. Hypervigilance was the setting her brain was jammed on. Watching out for danger, keeping alert to exploitation, always on guard against attack. Nope, it didn't make for a chilled-out personality. 'Hey, don't I get to ask you some questions?' she said.

'Not until I've asked mine.'

'That's not fair.' She threw in a pout for good measure. 'You're getting a head start.'

He smiled that half smile again as he pushed her bottom lip back in with the tip of his finger, like someone closing a drawer. 'Answer the question.'

Aiesha's lip tingled where he'd touched it. Tingled and burned. Ached. 'I hang out.'

'Hang out where?'

She gave a negligent shrug. 'The gym. The pool. The barre.'

His brows met over his nose. 'The bar?'

Aiesha rolled her eyes. 'Not *that* sort of bar. I do a ballet class. It's really good for posture and balance.'

His frown hadn't quite gone away but it wasn't one of disapproval, more one of intrigue. Maybe even a little respect. 'Where'd you go on your last holiday?'

'San Diego.'

'Who'd you go with?'

She hesitated for a brief second. 'I...I went alone. It's a pain having to travel with other people. They always want to see stuff you aren't interested in. I like being able to do what I want when I want.'

His eyes moved between each of hers for a lengthy pause. 'What happened in Vegas?'

Aiesha gave him a bored look. 'You don't need me to tell you. You read about it, didn't you? Everyone on the planet read it.'

'I want you to tell me your version of events.'

She looked at their joined hands, the way his tanned fingers contrasted with her paler ones. He had strong hands, artistic and clever. Hands that were trustworthy and honest. Clean hands.

Aiesha pulled out of his hold. 'He didn't tell me he was married.' The shame washed over her again. The fact that she hadn't recognised Antony made her feel foolish and naïve. That she'd allowed him to kiss her, to touch her, to get close to her shamed her. The fact that she'd gone up to his room made her feel ill. 'He wasn't wearing a ring. I had no idea he was married until his wife texted me.'

'How long were you involved with him?'

'Not long…'

'How long?'

She hugged her arms close to her body. 'I had dinner with him a couple of times after my shift. And no, contrary to what the press said, I didn't sleep with him.' But she'd been about to, which made her feel even more of a fool.

'The press showed you leaving his room,' James said.

Aiesha bristled when she thought of how Antony had allowed everyone to think *she* was the one who had done something wrong. In the past she would have relished being cast as the bad guy. During her adolescence she had planted herself in the middle of scandal after scandal, actively seeking negative press, the more outrageous the better. To her disordered way of thinking, it showed the world *someone* was interested in her.

But it was different now.

Over the last few months she had been planning her exit-Vegas strategy. She had become increasingly disenchanted with the life she was living. She lived and worked in one of the busiest and most fun places in the world and yet not a day went past when she didn't feel lonely and isolated and bored.

She was tired of the negativity associated with her image. Her tell-all interview about Clifford Challender had come back to bite her as the press had unearthed her history as a home-wrecker.

Now Antony had destroyed her attempt to make a fresh start. He had cast himself as the victim, the poor, misunderstood husband reeled in by an opportunistic seductress. But calling him out for a liar—even if anyone would've believed her, given her track record— would have hurt his wife and two school-age children. She had decided to disappear and let the dust settle instead.

'I went up to his room, but while I was in the bathroom I got a text message from his wife,' she said. 'I came out and told him what I thought of him and left.'

'That was a lucky shot for the press.'

'His wife tipped them off. She knew where he was and who he was with. The press did the rest.'

James was still frowning. 'You do realise by running away the way you did it made you look guilty?'

Aiesha shrugged again. 'It suited me to get out of Vegas.'

'But what will you do now?'

She gave him a worldly look. 'Find myself a sugar daddy or a rich husband. What else?'

A flicker of annoyance passed over his face. 'Be serious.'

'I *am* being serious.' She stepped closer and tiptoed her fingers down his chest. 'How about it, James? You fancy hiring me full-time as your wife? I'll give good value for money. You can do whatever you want with me—' she smiled her tartiest smile '—for the right price.'

He captured her hand, holding it in a firm grip. 'I know what you're doing.'

Aiesha brushed her pelvis against his. This was much better. This was the language she was used to. Sex was much easier to handle than emotional intimacy. He already thought her an outrageous tart. The entire world thought it…and to some degree the world was right. She had been flirtatious and provocative to get where she was, even though she no longer wanted to be there. Why not make the most of his bad opinion of her?

'What am I doing, posh boy?'

His jaw flickered with a pulse as if his self-control was only just holding. But she could see the naked flare of lust in his dark blue gaze. 'You're hiding behind that sex-kitten mask you like wearing. It's not who you are. It's just a game you play.'

Aiesha laughed off his assessment of her but she worried he had seen too much. Knew too much. Sensed too much. She prided herself on being hard to read. No one got under her guard. No one ambushed her emotionally.

Not even smarmy Antony had engaged her emotions. She had seen him as a means to an end—a first class ticket out of Vegas.

But James Challender wasn't like other men. He was not easily manipulated. He didn't lie and cheat and lather on the charm to get his own way.

He didn't fight dirty.

He didn't play dirty.

She wanted to keep things physical between them but he kept pushing against her emotional armour. He wanted to uncover her. To expose her. To know her. The thought terrified her. Opening up to someone, laying it all bare was what weak people did. She was strong. Resilient. Self-sufficient. She relied on her wits and her body to get where she wanted to go. Her heart was not up for sale. 'You like playing, too, don't you, James? You want to play *so* bad.'

His eyes dipped to her mouth. She could read the battle playing out on his face. He wanted her but he was fighting it every step of the way. He took a deep breath and dropped his hold as he stepped back from her. 'I'm going out.'

'But it's snowing.'

He gave her a black look over his shoulder as he left. 'Good.'

James drew in a deep draught of icy air but it didn't do much to quell the fire of wanting burning in his flesh. It was like trying to extinguish a wind-driven wildfire by spitting on it. Aiesha was living, breathing dynamite when she put her mind and body to it. He was hanging on to his self-control by a gossamer thread. He had never wanted anyone the way he wanted her. It was all he could think of—how he wanted her. Ached for her. Needed her. Hungered for her. Every sultry look she gave him made him throb with intense longing. She was the ultimate tease, ramping up his need every chance she could, switching tactics so deftly he didn't know what to expect from her next. Temptress or doe-eyed innocent. Wild-child whore or lost waif. She did them all so well.

Last night had revealed a tiny chink in her armour but she was back to business now. He didn't like being played. He didn't like being a pawn in one of her mischief-making games. She got way too much power by playing the vamp. He had tried to get under her guard, to see the girl behind the mask, but she had pulled the curtain on him.

But he had seen enough to make him want to see more.

She had no close friends. She holidayed alone. She had taken the rap for a scandal caused by a wandering husband who couldn't keep his hands to himself. She had lost her job and pretended it didn't matter.

She composed music that was hauntingly beautiful for someone who had clearly meant a great deal to her....

Had anyone else heard that poignant piece of music? The depth of emotion in those few bars he'd heard had stopped him in his tracks. He could have listened to her for hours. She had looked so absorbed, so in the moment, she'd seemed to be lost in an internal world in which the music was somehow translating emotions she dared not or would not voice aloud. Those rising and falling cadences, those heartstring-pulling minor chords were still playing in his head, moving him, and haunting him still. The way the rhythm flowed, paused, and flowed again. But he had a feeling that particular piece was something she kept private. Why else had she looked so annoyed when he'd disturbed her?

There was so much about Aiesha he didn't know. There was so much she kept hidden.

There was so much he wanted to discover.

She was complicated and contrary. Beguiling and bewitching and beautiful and bold and brazen. Maddening.

And yet...likeable.

His instincts had been right. She had been genuinely upset after her knockout blow to his nose. Even though she tried her best to hide it, her gaze kept going to his black eye with a little flicker of concern. He saw the way she chewed at the inside of her mouth when she thought he wasn't looking. The way she deliberately tried to seduce him, but then pulled back whenever he took the lead. What was that all about?

James turned up his coat collar against the snow. He shoved his hands into his pockets and frowned.

It would be dangerous but he would have to get even closer to her to find out.

CHAPTER SEVEN

Aiesha was trying to get to Archie in time... She was running as hard and as fast as she could but her legs were useless, powerless. They were shaking so much they felt as if they were made of overcooked spaghetti. Fear clotted the blood in her veins, it stole the oxygen from her lungs, it churned her stomach contents, liquefied and soured them in panic. She got a little closer. But then she stumbled over someone's skateboard, fell to her knees, her arms reaching out, her voice hoarse from screaming, 'Noooo!'

Aiesha sat bolt upright in bed, her throat raw from gasping and her chest pounding so hard she could hear the echo of it in her ears. The sound of her ragged breathing was deafening in the dead silence of the night.

She hadn't screamed out loud...or at least she didn't think so. Her room was a fair distance from James's and there was no sound of him stirring. There was no sound of a door opening. No footsteps running down the passage. No voice calling out to see if she was all right.

She waited in the darkness, poised, tense, agitated. Long minutes passed.

She lay back down and closed her eyes but it was impossible to relax, let alone sleep with those horrible images flickering behind her eyelids like an old black-and-white film set on permanent replay.

Aiesha threw off the bedcovers and reached for her wrap. A hot drink with a shot of brandy would have to do as James might not appreciate hearing her running through her scales at this hour. She hadn't seen him since he'd found her playing Archie's song earlier that day. But she could still feel the impact of his kiss reverberating through her body like the humming of a tuning fork.

When she got to the kitchen, Bonnie got up off her bed and looked up at Aiesha with a sheepish look in her brown eyes, her feathery tail slowly wagging back and forth like a metronome on three-two time.

'Don't even think about it,' Aiesha said and reached for the fridge handle. 'You'll have to cross your legs or something.'

The dog gave a little whine and padded towards the back door, looking back over her shoulder as if to say, *Come on—what's taking you so long?*

Aiesha closed the fridge and put the milk carton on the counter with a muttered curse. 'How come you don't use a pet door? I thought golden retrievers were supposed to be smart? You're the dumbest one I've met.'

She opened the back door, wincing as a blast of the icy wind whipped it back against the wall. The dog ambled out, sniffing the ground as she went, looking as if she had all the time in the world. 'Will you hurry up?' Aiesha said, shivering as the wind skirted around her bare ankles. 'Hey, don't go out of sight. I'm not going looking for you.'

The dog disappeared behind the low hedge that surrounded the vegetable garden. Aiesha swore under her breath as she reached for a jacket hanging by the door. She could smell Louise's perfume on it and for a moment she felt as if it were Louise herself wrapping her arms around her as she slipped her arms through the sleeves.

She stood for a moment in the darkness, wondering what life would have been like with Louise as her mother. Her music would have been celebrated, encouraged, nurtured… She would have been loved, celebrated, encouraged.

She would have been safe.

She looked up at the night sky, the sprinkling of stars and planets like peepholes in a dark blue velvet blanket. How many times as a child had she looked up there and wished upon a star? Wished for her life to be different? For everything to change?

She sighed and stuffed her feet into a pair of Louise's boots by the door. But before she had taken two steps the howling wind whipped around again and slammed the door behind her.

'*Shoot!*'

James woke to the sound of a door slamming. He thought he'd locked up everything securely on his last round downstairs. But the house was old and the wind was gale force so it didn't surprise him that a catch had come loose. He shrugged on a robe and went downstairs. Aiesha's bedroom door was closed and there was no light on, which meant Sleeping Beauty was fast asleep. He hoped.

When he got to the back door off the kitchen he could hear frantic knocking and swearing. He opened the door to find a shivering Aiesha on the doorstep. She was dressed in one of his mother's jackets with the hood pulled up over her head. Her body was quaking with cold but her eyes were blazing. She pushed past him with a savage imprecation. 'Took you long enough.' She stomped snow all over the floor. 'That stupid dog needs a tracking device. *You* go and find her. I'm frozen stiff.'

James caught the jacket midair before it landed on the floor where she'd kicked off the boots. She was in a towering rage, which seemed out of proportion to the circumstances. 'She won't stay out long in this wind,' he said. 'I didn't hear her barking to be let out. Did she wake you?'

'No, I was…already awake.'

Something about her expression was suddenly furtive. Secretive. What had she been doing downstairs in the middle of the night? He narrowed his gaze. She was backed against the kitchen counter, her chin at that defiant height, her cheeks pink from cold or guilt, or both. Suspicion crawled along his skin. Was she putting away a stash of his mother's jewellery or other valuables for when she left? A little bit here, a little bit there, hiding it away in incremental bits so as not to be detected.

The back of his neck prickled in anger. So this was how she was going to repay his mother for her kindness, was it?

'What were you doing downstairs at this time of night?'

The pink in her cheeks went a shade darker but her eyes remained diamond-hard. 'I was getting a drink.'

His gaze briefly went to the milk on the bench. 'Is that all?' he asked.

Her brows snapped together and the pink in her cheeks turned red. Angry red. Defensive red. 'What do you mean, "Is that all?" What—do you think I'm pilfering the silver while you sleep?' Her eyes flashed at him, her mouth flattening in a whitened line. 'Why don't you check each drawer to see if I've pinched any of your precious heirlooms?'

She started marching about the kitchen like an angry cop armed with a long-awaited search warrant. Opening cupboards wildly, banging doors, pulling out drawers with savage jerks of her hands. There was an air of mania about her. Of hysteria about to erupt. She pulled open the silverware drawer of the oak sideboard so quickly the contents landed in a clattering, deafening heap on the floor.

She stood looking at the jumbled mess of his mother's silverware in frozen silence.

And then, right in front of his eyes, she started to crack. It was like watching an ice sculpture fracture, centimetre by centimetre. Her eyes darted and flickered. Her tongue dashed out over her lips. Her stiff angry posture faltered. Her shoulders trembled. Her torso folded. 'I'm sorry...' She swallowed and dropped to her knees and began to reach for the silverware but he could see her hands were shaking almost uncontrollably and she barely managed to pick up a teaspoon before it dropped with a ping to the floor.

He crouched down beside her and put a hand over her trembling one. 'Leave it.'

Her eyes were trained on his chin as if she couldn't bring herself to meet his gaze, but her tone was resentful and snarly. 'Don't you want to count them?'

Something about her attempt to sound defiant when she was clearly so upset touched him. Ambushed him. She reminded him of a kitten puffing its fur up to look tough against a big scary dog. 'It can wait.' He searched her expression for a moment. 'Hey, are you OK?'

There was a whining at the back door and Aiesha's mask slipped back on like a glove. 'You'd better get that. Can't have your mother's dog carking it while she's under your protection, can you?'

It only took James five seconds to let the dog in but when he turned around Aiesha had disappeared.

Aiesha leant heavily on her bedroom door with bated breath, waiting for the sound of James's footsteps along the passage. Her heart thudded as each long second passed. What was he thinking of her after that crazy little show? What was he thinking of her brash attitude now she had let it slip? He had seen her at her worst. Out of control. Panicked. Upset. Vulnerable. She had lost it in front of him. She'd acted like some screwed-up nut job, throwing the contents of the kitchen around like one of her creepy mother's boyfriends in a drunken tantrum.

Would he mock her? Laugh at her?

Or, worse, would he try and understand her? *Know* her?

Aiesha thought of telling him...of finally being able to share some of the pain she carried like toxic waste in her bones. The shame of her childhood, the sense of being an outsider, the one no one wanted. The crushing weight of guilt she felt about not being able to protect her mother and Archie. The niggling despair that she might never be able to get her life on track. To reach her potential instead of being stymied by her past. How would James react to finding out she was not as tough as she made everyone think? That, underneath the brash facade, she was as sensitive and caring as his mother? Maybe even more so...

She heard the stairs creak as he came up them. She heard each of his footsteps, unhurried, steady and sure. She heard him pause outside her bedroom door. Heard the deep gravel-rough baritone of his voice. 'Aiesha?'

She clamped her teeth together to stop from calling out to him. She didn't need his comfort. She didn't need anyone's comfort. She had been on her own for the last ten years—for most of her life—and that was the way it was going to stay. So what if she'd got a little panicked over losing the dog in the dark? Big deal. The dog came back. No harm done.

The silence stretched and stretched and stretched along with her held breath. Aiesha wasn't sure which would break first—the silence or her lungs.

'Can we talk?' James said.

She clenched her hands into tight balls of self-containment. *No. Go away.*

'What I implied downstairs...' he paused momentarily '...it was uncalled for. I'm sorry.'

Another endless silence passed.

Then she heard him give a long sigh, as if he, too, had been holding his breath too long.

And then she heard the sound of his footsteps as he went further along the passage to his room, and then the soft click of his door closing.

Aiesha squeezed her eyes shut to stop the blinding stinging tears from escaping.

She. Would. Not. Cry.

When Aiesha looked out of the kitchen window the next morning she saw James clearing the driveway with a shovel. There had been a new fall of snow overnight but the sun was out and shining brightly, giving the wintry scene a sparkling brilliance that was blinding. James looked strong and lean as he loaded each shovel with snow and tossed it aside. He had taken off his coat and worked in his shirt and sweater. Even through the layers of fabric she could see the play of his muscles. He wasn't the gym-rat type but he still looked good. Damn good. He dug the shovel in the snow again and again, tossing its load to the side in a mechanical fashion, his brow deeply furrowed as if he was mulling over something…her, most probably.

Was he thinking she was a tantrum-throwing child in a woman's body? Was he thinking she was in need of a psychiatrist's couch? Was he thinking she was in need of a straitjacket?

She gritted her teeth. Best to get it over with. No point hiding away from him. If he mocked her then she would mock him right on back.

She pulled on her coat and mittens and wrapped a scarf around her neck. The cold air hit her face like the slap of an icy hand across her cheeks. She drew the scarf closer and wandered over to where James was shovelling with such vigour. 'Looking for my buried stash?'

He stopped shovelling to look at her with a rueful expression. 'I suppose I deserve that.' His eyes moved over her face as if searching for something. 'Are you OK?'

She made her gaze as direct and steely as she could. 'Never better.'

He gave a slow nod, which she took as an acknowledgement of her decision not to mention her meltdown episode last night. He went back to the task at hand, shovelling the snow. *Shoosh. Whoosh. Plop.* Spade after spade. Aiesha got the impression he was trying to distract himself from her presence. Did she disgust him? Did she repulse him with her out-of-control behaviour? Was that why he was keeping himself so busy? He didn't want to be with her. He didn't desire her now he knew how childish she could be. *Fine.*

'The forecast is improving,' he said without looking her way. 'We should be out of here by Friday. Maybe even earlier if the snowploughs come this way.'

She folded her arms. '*We?*'

He paused his shovelling to look at her. 'You'll have to come with me to Paris. I have a meeting with a client.'

She frowned at him. 'Hang on a minute. You said you were coming up here for a week and that what's-her-name was joining you at the weekend. Why the sudden rush off to Paris?'

'My client wants to go over the plans I've drawn up.'

'Why can't you email them to him?'

'He prefers to meet in person,' he said. 'He's old-fashioned that way. Besides, he wants to meet you.'

'Why on earth would he want to meet me?'

His look was still inscrutable. 'You're my fiancée, remember?' He went back to shovelling. 'We'll stay at a boutique hotel in Montmartre. There's a fund-raising dinner being held there for one of the charities my client is involved in.'

Aiesha swallowed a mouthful of panic. Staying in a hotel. One suite. One bed. *All night*. What if she had another nightmare? What if she…?

'I'm not going. I want to stay here. I hate Paris.' Romantic couples everywhere, walking hand in hand through the city of love. It was enough to make her want to puke.

He leaned on the handle of the shovel, his eyes meeting hers. 'You're the one who kicked this charade off. By the way, I did an electronic transfer of the funds into your bank account last night. Think of this as a job. You and I are engaged until such time as I call it off.'

He wanted to call the tune now, did he? Well, she was going to call her own. She planted her hands on her hips, straightened her shoulders and upped her chin. 'I want my own room.'

He stabbed the spade in the snow again. 'That would cause way too much speculation.' He tossed the snow before he gave her a crooked smile. 'Can't have everyone tweeting about that, can we?'

Aiesha threw him a caustic glare. 'I always sleep alone. I hate sharing a bed. I hate being disturbed by someone snoring or groping me when I'm trying to sleep.'

He leaned on his shovel to look at her with that penetrative gaze of his. 'Do you often have trouble sleeping?'

She tried to keep her game face on but she could feel it crumbling around the edges. 'Just because I get up to get a drink now and again doesn't mean I'm an insomniac. This house makes a lot of noise at night. It's creepy.'

He continued to study her, his gaze unwavering. 'Just as well I'm here with you to keep you safe from all the ghosts and ghouls then, isn't it?'

Was he mocking her? It was hard to tell from his expression. She let go of the inside of her lip and changed the subject. 'What about the dog? Who's going to look after it?'

'Mrs McBain has a nephew who said he'd take care of her for a couple of days.'

Aiesha tried another tack. 'I promised your mother I would do it. She was relying on me to house-sit until she gets back because Mrs McBain wanted to visit her daughter in Yorkshire. I don't want to let her down. Not after all she's done for me.'

His look was still searching. 'Have you heard from her since she left?'

Aiesha rolled her lips together. She hadn't heard a peep from his mother. She couldn't decide if Louise was annoyed with her or too preoccupied with worry over her friend's health to be concerned with what was going on—or not going on—at home. 'No, but I'm sure it's because she's busy looking after her friend. She might be in a remote area or something without a proper signal for her phone.'

'Do you think she cooked this up?' He pointed to her and then back at himself. 'You and me, stuck here together like this?'

Aiesha gave an uncomfortable little laugh. 'Surely you don't think your mother has the ability to summon up a blizzard to suit her own ends? And why on earth would she want you and me to hook up? She knows how much we dislike each other.'

Those dark blue eyes were still holding hers in a lock that made her spine feel like molten wax. 'What if she's playing fairy godmother?' he said. 'Waving her magic wand around to make everything turn out the way she wants it.'

'I hardly think your mother wants a Vegas lounge singer as her future daughter-in-law,' Aiesha said, trying to ignore the strange little pang below her heart. If her circumstances were different, Louise was exactly the sort of mother-in-law she would've liked....

'She has a soft spot for you. She always has.'

Aiesha kicked a little mound of snow away with the toe of her boot. 'Doesn't mean she wants me to be the mother of her grandkids.'

His gaze flicked to her abdomen as if imagining her swollen with his child. When his eyes reconnected with hers Aiesha felt her cheeks grow warm and her heart gave a funny little jolting movement that all but snatched her breath away.

James would be a wonderful father. He would be upright and steady, reliable and sensible. Kind and loving.

He would be patient and yet firm. He would take the time to understand his children, to get to know them. He would provide for them and never exploit or abuse them or the trust they had in him.

A vision slipped under a barrier inside her head…a vision of James holding a newborn baby. A tiny pink, dimpled little baby with scrunched-up eyes and a rose-bud mouth. Ten tiny fingers, ten wriggling toes, a little button nose and ears like miniature shells.

Something tightly wound up inside her belly began to loosen, unravel. Break free. Could James see the nascent longing she was fighting so hard to hide? The longing she hardly realised she possessed until now. It was a hunger that was buried so deep inside her she hadn't heard its voice above the babble of activity with which she had filled her life thus far.

The yearning she had for a family she could call her own.

To belong.

To be part of a family unit that was so strong noth-ing and no one could ever break it apart.

To be loved and to love in return.

Aiesha berated herself for her silly little pipe dreams, for those ridiculously fanciful imaginings that had no foothold in the real world. What sort of mother would *she* make? She couldn't even keep a dog safe from harm.

She swung away to go back to the house. 'I'm going to have breakfast.'

'How about making me some?'

She threw him a frosty look over her shoulder. 'Make it yourself.'

* * *

James came into the warm kitchen where Aiesha was sitting huddled over a mug of tea. She gave him a sideways glance that was two parts glower and went back to staring at her tea. He looked at the bowl of porridge she had set aside on the cooker and gave a private smile. He was right. She was not as tough on the inside as she showed on the outside. It was all bluster and posturing. She had a soft heart but it was hidden where no one could reach it.

Last night had shown him how much she cared. She had been genuinely worried about Bonnie going missing. She had come flouncing in with her usual you-fix-it-it's-not-my-problem manner but it was all bluff. She had acted childishly under pressure but rather than mock her for it, he felt drawn to her. She brought out every protective instinct he possessed. Getting to know her was proving to be the most fascinating and moving experience of his life.

What would it take for her to trust him enough to drop the mask? Would she ever feel safe enough to show her true self? Or would he have to be satisfied with rare glimpses, leaving him feeling frustrated and manipulated and dissatisfied?

'Is this for me?' he asked.

'I made too much.' Another hard little glare. 'No point wasting perfectly good food.'

He pulled out a chair and sat opposite her. 'Stop scowling at me. It's ruining my appetite.'

Her fingers fidgeted with the handle of her mug. She had slender fingers, with nails that were short but neatly manicured. The first two of her knuckles on her right hand were faintly bruised. His chest felt strangely tight, as if someone was turning a spanner on each of the valves of his heart. He hadn't realised she'd hurt herself when she'd landed him with that punch the other night. She hadn't said a word.

So many layers…

So many secrets…

'Is your hand OK? It looks bruised. Did you—?'

She slipped her right hand beneath the table. 'It's fine. I bumped it against something.'

'Aiesha.'

She gave him the sort of look an unrepentant delinquent did a correction officer. 'What?'

'Give me your hand.'

She looked as if she was going to refuse his command, but then she rolled her eyes and shoved her hand out to him. He took her hand gently in his and began brushing his thumb over the back of it. Nothing moved on her face but he felt her fingers shift inside the cup of his, a soft little trembling movement that made his body spring to attention. His groin throbbed as he remembered how those fingers had wrapped around him. Holding him. Caressing him until he had to fight every instinct to explode. She was blowing cold on him now but how long before she switched back to sultry siren? She was so complex, so deeply layered, like a lake or a pond that had hidden caves and canyons below the surface.

James released her hand and sat back and picked up his spoon. 'We need to get you a ring.'

She blinked at him. 'What?'

He pointed to her left hand with his spoon. 'An engagement ring.'

And, bang on cue, she did it.

One of her slim eyebrows arched and her grey eyes sparkled with her usual cheekiness. 'Do I get to keep it after we break up?'

'Sure.' He sprinkled some more brown sugar on his porridge. 'Think of it as a consolation prize.'

There was a moment of silence.

'It's not the one you bought for Phoebe what's-her-face, is it?'

He looked up from his breakfast to give her a lazy smile. 'No point wasting a perfectly good diamond.'

Her eyes hardened as she leaned across the table and pushed his spoon down away from his mouth. 'Listen up. I don't wear other women's cast-offs. Got it?'

James felt the tingle of her touch run all the way up his arm. The fire in her gaze lit a blaze in his pelvis. He could feel the blood surging through his veins, thickening him with lust that was like a raging fever. Her mouth was set in an intractable line but it still looked lush and plump. It was impossible for such a beautiful mouth to look anything else. He remembered the taste of her, sweet and hot and sinful. Her tongue swift and seductive as it mated with his. He wanted to feel her tongue, hot and wet, on his neck, on his chest, his abdomen, stroking and licking all the way down to where he throbbed the hardest.

'I'm not wasting my money on a ring you'll only be

wearing for a couple of weeks,' he said. 'What would be the point?'

She pushed back her chair and got up from the table. 'Fine. Whatever.'

James frowned as he watched her stalk over to put her mug in the dishwasher. 'What's wrong?'

She slammed the dishwasher door. 'Nothing.'

He rose from the table and went over to where she was standing with her arms folded across her body. Her expression was stormy and resentful and her eyes marble-hard.

'What does it matter what ring you wear when all of this is a sham?' he asked.

Her eyes glittered at they met his. 'Do you know how insulting it is to be given something that was intended for someone else?'

'Are we talking about engagement rings or something else?'

Her chin came up. 'What else could we be talking about?'

'Who gave you something that was meant for someone else?'

'No one.'

He studied her expression for a moment, watching as her grey eyes locked him out as surely as if a shutter had come down. 'Talk to me, Aiesha.'

'About what?'

He stroked a fingertip along the curve of her jaw, from just below her ear to her chin, but surprisingly she didn't jerk away. 'Tell me why you're upset.'

'I'm not upset.' Her lips barely moved as she spoke. 'I'm angry.'

James quirked an eyebrow. 'Angry about a few days in Paris, all expenses paid?'

She pursed her lips, firing another glare at him. 'I packed in a hurry to get here. I don't have the right clothes to wear.'

He stroked the underside of her chin, pushing it up so her embittered gaze couldn't escape his. 'So I'll buy you some clothes while we're in Paris. That's what sugar daddies and rich fiancés do, isn't it?'

'How are you going to explain that black eye to your business friend?'

James had wondered that himself. 'I'll tell him I walked into a door.'

Her look was scathing. 'Not very original.'

'Any ideas?'

Something shifted in her gaze, a fleeting shadow, but then she was back to her street-smart sass. 'I could give you some concealer to put on. Or I could do it for you. I'm a bit of an expert. Bruises are pretty easy to disguise. Cuts and swelling less so.'

He frowned. 'You've used concealer before? For covering bruises and cuts?'

'I should've been a make-up artist.' Her tone had a cynical edge to it. 'I had a long apprenticeship patching up my mother from all her sicko boyfriends beating her up. Should've put that on my CV. I wonder if it's too late for a career change?'

James's stomach contents churned, his heart contracting in disgust at what she must have witnessed.

At what her mother must have suffered. 'Did any of them hit you?'

She pushed her tongue into the side of her cheek before she answered. 'Couple of times.'

He swallowed a mouthful of bile. He thought of her as a child, all skinny legs and arms, being assaulted by someone huge and threatening. How could she possibly have defended herself? Violence in general was abhorrent to him, but violence against women and children sickened him to the core. Was that why she was so restless at night? What horrors had she locked away in her mind? What abuse had she seen or experienced first-hand?

'Is that why you ran away from home?'

She directed her gaze to the left lapel of his collar. He saw her draw in a breath, hold it for a beat, before slowly releasing it. 'A couple of days after my mother died of a heroin overdose, nobly supplied by her latest de facto, he decided I would make a good substitute in his bed. I declined.'

James swallowed thickly. Painfully. 'He tried to… to rape you?'

She didn't meet his gaze but kept staring at his lapel. 'I got out before it came to that.'

'So that's why you ran away.'

She nodded. 'Yep.'

James sensed there was more to it than that but she wasn't saying. He could read her better now. She put on that shield of brash armour, the tough-girl exterior that hid a world of pain. He heard it in the tone of her voice. He saw it in the brittleness of her eyes. It was a barrier she put up to make people back off from getting too close to her. She was like a junkyard dog, all bluster and bluff for self-protection. 'How long were you on the streets?'

'I couch surfed for a few nights but people soon get sick of freeloaders.'

'But you were fifteen, for God's sake!'

She shrugged. 'Yeah, well, they say charity begins at home but it wasn't at any of the homes I stayed in... except maybe your mum's.'

James frowned harder. 'Then why did you sabotage your stay with her?'

She met his gaze then. Hers was hard as steel. Cordoned off. Impenetrable. 'Your father was cheating on her. I overheard him talking to his mistress. I decided to show your mum what type of man he was. She deserves better. Much better.'

James looked at her in puzzlement. 'But surely you could've handled it without involving the press. You hurt my mother more than you hurt my father.' *And me.*

She gave another careless shrug of her shoulders. 'As you say, I was fifteen. I didn't know any better at the time.'

'What about the jewellery?' he asked. 'You do realise you could've been charged with theft if my mother hadn't pretended it was a gift?'

The tight set to her mouth softened a fraction. 'Yeah, well, I sent it back to her after I got paid for my story.'

James looked at her in a combination of frustration and admiration. She was a survivor. She fought her corner and fought hard. She used whatever weapons she had at her disposal. Wit. Charm. Artifice. Seduction. She was wily, as cunning as a vixen and as cute as a kitten, whichever suited her needs best.

But underneath all that he could see something else. *Someone* else. Someone who didn't let anyone get too close. Someone who didn't trust others not to exploit her or harm her. Someone who felt more than she cared to show.

'You said your mother died. What about your father?'

'I haven't seen him since I was eight.'

'His choice or yours?'

She gave him another cynical look. 'Her Majesty's choice.'

'He's in prison?'

'Yep.'

'For?'

'For being a jerk.'

James let it go. She clearly didn't want to talk about it. He was surprised she had told him what she had. He wondered if his mother had got as much out of her. He felt annoyed with himself for not understanding Aiesha better. Was that why his mother had resumed contact? She had understood there was much more to that brooding teenager with the challenging behaviour. His mother had seen the potential inside Aiesha to become a beautiful swan if only she had a chance to shine. She was not used to letting people in. His mother had been patient, spending the last eight years keeping in contact with Aiesha, letting her know there was a safe haven for her if ever she needed it.

'You don't have to feel ashamed of where you've

come from, Aiesha,' he said. 'None of that was your choice.'

She pushed her lips out in a what-would-you-know manner. 'I'm going to have a shower. Talking about my background always makes me feel dirty.'

Aiesha was still agitated after her shower. She stood staring out of the window at the whitened fields and forest, wondering why she had told James so much. She wasn't used to talking about her past. She *never* talked about it. Not to anyone. She'd didn't want people to think any less of her for being the daughter of a criminal and a heroin addict. She had spent most of her life trying to hide it.

It was hardly something you brought up as small talk at a cocktail party: *What does my father do, you ask? He's a career criminal. Armed robbery and assault with a deadly weapon. Drugs. Breaking and entering. You name it. He's either done it or has a mate who has.*

Aiesha had always been the outsider at school. The one everyone pointed at, whispered about, gossiped about. She had learned early on to mask her feelings, to armour up so no one knew how much those snarky comments hurt. But it had hurt to be the only one not invited to another child's birthday party. It had hurt to be the last one picked for a team. It had hurt to walk out of the school gate and see all the other mothers or fathers gathered to collect their children while there was no one waiting for her.

Her high-school parent–teacher interviews were the worst. Her mother would make an effort to sober up

and drag herself there but Aiesha wished she hadn't
bothered. The pitying looks that came her way from
the teachers afterwards only intensified her feelings
of being an outcast.

But then one day a couple of weeks before her fif-
teenth birthday she found Archie.

It was still the best day of her life. She had found
him near the tube station close to where she and her
mother and the Beast Man lived. They weren't supposed to have pets in the flat but Aiesha smuggled him
in and out under her coat. He was terrier-small but of
mixed breeding with a face only a mother could love.
She didn't know how old Archie was or where he had
come from, but from the moment he'd come over to her
and looked up at her plaintively with those big brown
eyes and wagged his tail she was smitten.

Archie would trot along to school with her each day
and wait patiently in the alley behind the dry-cleaner's
shop until she returned each afternoon. It was the high-
light of her day to see him waiting for her there. His
head would come up off his paws and his eyes would
brighten and that stumpy little tail would wag so hard
Aiesha was sure one day it would fall off. She would
give him the scraps she'd saved from her school dinner and then they would walk to the park, where she
would pretend she was like all the other dog-owners.
Going home to a nice house with a garden, warm and
cosy in winter, cool and smelling of flowers in summer. To food, not just on the table but also in the pan-
try and in the fridge. To a mother who wasn't stoned or
drunk or beaten within an inch of her life. To a father—

or stepfather—who wasn't sending her leering looks through piggy eyes and smacking his thick wet lips at her.

Why had she told James—of all people—about her horrible background? How was she supposed to keep her emotions out of their relationship if he kept getting her to divulge stuff she had never spoken of to anyone before? Was it his steadiness? His centred calm that she envied so much? His self-control? His concern? His compassion?

Aiesha was used to being judged and vilified. Mocked and berated and excluded. She wasn't used to being listened to. She wasn't used to being understood. She wasn't used to showing a side of herself that had been hidden away since childhood. How would she re-assemble her armour if pieces of it were missing? The breastplate over her heart was no longer a thick layer of metal. It felt like a flimsy sheet of baking paper.

James would only have to hold her too close to the warm, firm safe shelter of his body and it would be totally destroyed....

CHAPTER EIGHT

'SO YOU'VE FINALLY decided to answer your phone,' James said to his mother later that night. 'What the hell do you think you're up to?'

'I could ask you the very same question, darling,' Louise countered. 'You're not really engaged to Aiesha, are you?'

'Of course not, but for God's sake don't tell Dad that. I let him think it was genuine…along with the rest of the world.'

'Your little secret is safe with me.'

James frowned at his mother's amused tone. 'You must've realised something like this would happen.'

'I had no idea you were planning to visit me,' his mother said. 'Last time we spoke, you said you were behind on the terribly important project you were working on and couldn't possibly spare the time to drive all that way just to—'

'So I'm a little task oriented at times,' he said, cutting off his mother's you-work-too-hard lecture. 'You'd be worried if I was lazing on some Caribbean beach with a bikini model half my age like someone else we know. Why didn't you tell me Aiesha was here?'

'You know why.'

He let the recriminating silence pass. Yes, he could be stubborn. Yes, he could be unforgiving when someone crossed him. But that didn't mean his mother should have kept her relationship with Aiesha a secret for all this time. She should have told him so he could have handled things a little better. He'd blundered in like a clumsy clown in a china shop. He didn't like the feeling. He was used to being in control. He was used to taking strategic measures to sort out difficult problems, not make them a hundred times worse.

'You don't know her, James,' his mother said. 'You don't know her the way I do. You've done what everyone else does when they meet her. They take her on face value and don't see the sweetheart of a girl hiding behind that don't-mess-with-me facade.'

James had seen the sweetheart girl; trouble was, he didn't know what to do with her. Well, he knew what he *wanted* to do with her. It was a constant ache to get on and do it. An overwhelming temptation he was finding very hard to resist. Wasn't sure he *could* resist. 'You still should've given me the heads-up on her being here. You know how much I hate surprises.'

'I hope you haven't been unkind to her.'

He gave an ironic bark of laughter. 'Unkind? I'm the one currently sporting a black eye.'

'Oh, my goodness! What happened?'

'You know that saying, "let sleeping dogs lie"? I should've taken note.'

Louise sighed. 'I'm sure she didn't mean it.'

James swung his chair so he could look at the moon rising over the tops of the forest trees. Australia suddenly seemed a very long way away. Another world away. A world without five feet eight of temptation torturing his every waking moment. 'When are you coming back?'

'Erm…darling, there's something I want to tell you but I don't want you to be upset.'

He swung his chair back round, his right hand gripping the armrest. 'You're not thinking of emigrating, are you?'

'No, darling, nothing like that.' He heard her take a quick breath before she added, 'I'm seeing someone.'

'Seeing someone as in *seeing* someone?' James said.

His mother gave an embarrassed laugh. 'You sound just like your grandfather when I was a teenager going out on my first date. Please don't be cross. I'm happy for the first time in years.'

'Who is it?'

'Julie's brother, Richard,' she said. 'I've known him for decades. Actually, I knew him before I met your father. He was involved with someone else back then, and then your father came along and…well, you know how that turned out. Anyway, Richard flew out from Manchester to be with Julie after her accident and… well…we've fallen in love.'

His mother? *In love?* 'How well do you know this guy?' he asked. 'You haven't seen him for years. What if he's turned into some wacko weirdo on the make who just wants you for your money? Come on, Mum, think about this for a bit. You can't just rush into a relation-ship without giving it some careful thought.'

'Like you gave it so much careful thought before you decided Phoebe was the one you wanted to marry?'

James frowned. 'I didn't tell you I was going to marry Phoebe.'

'You didn't need to,' Louise said. 'I figured it out for myself. She's totally wrong for you. I'm surprised you can't see it for yourself.'

He rolled his chair back and stood. 'I'm starting to smell a very big meddlesome rat.'

'I had nothing to do with what's happened,' she said. 'But maybe the universe is trying to tell you some-thing. Don't ruin your life by marrying someone you don't love when I know the way you're capable of lov-ing someone. Don't love with part of yourself, James. Love with *all* of yourself.'

James paced the floor, his fingers clamped on his phone so tightly the tendons in his wrist protested. 'Look, this engagement with Aiesha isn't the real deal. I hope you understand that? It'll be over as soon as I get this project with Howard Sherwood finalised.'

'Of course it will.'

'I'm not in love with her.'

'Of course not, darling.'

James frowned again at his mother's disingenuous tone. 'Don't get any funny ideas.'

'Darling, you're *so* cynical. I didn't orchestrate poor Julie to run her car off the road. And I certainly didn't have anything to do with the weather. Aiesha needed a place to stay and I welcomed her. The fact that I didn't mention it to you is neither here nor there. I don't tell you every time I invite someone to stay with me. But would you like me to do so in future?'

'Now you're being ridiculous.'

Louise gave a confessional-sounding sigh. 'Look, I must admit I've always secretly hoped you would one day have some face-to-face time with her, even if it was only for a few minutes. You haven't seen her for a decade. It's surely time to move on? The fact that you got stranded together is a good thing. It's like it was meant to be.'

'Have you been drinking?'

'Darling, you can be so terribly stubborn at times. You made up your mind about Aiesha years ago when she was a troubled teenager. That's not who she is now. I suspect that's not who she ever was. Please be nice to her.'

James wondered what his mother would say if she knew just *how* nice he was being to Aiesha. Nice enough to hold her. To kiss her. To want to make love to her so badly his whole body throbbed with it. 'I'm taking her to Paris with me. Is that nice enough for you?'

'Lovely,' Louise said. 'I knew you'd sort out your differences eventually. Now, will you be nice to Richard when I introduce you to him?'

'When do I get the chance to give him the once-over?' James asked.

'We'll have to have a double date or something when we get home,' Louise said. 'Won't that be fun?'

He rolled his eyes. 'An absolute riot.'

Aiesha was flicking through the channels on the television in the sitting room when James came striding in with a brooding frown on his face. 'My mother has hooked up with some guy and fancies herself in love with him. Can you believe that? She knew him years ago but she's only seen him for a few days since and now she thinks she's in love. Unbelievable. Freaking unbelievable.'

'Aw...how sweet.'

He glared at her. 'This is my mother we're talking about, not some young girl with stars in her eyes. She's fifty-nine years old, for God's sake. She should have more sense.'

Aiesha put the remote control on the ottoman before she got up from the sofa. 'Just because she's middle-aged doesn't mean she's dead from the waist down.'

His brows were jammed together over his eyes. 'What's that supposed to mean?'

She eased her hair out of the back of her sweater, shaking it free over her shoulders as she held his narrowed gaze. 'Sex.'

He sent a hand through his already tousled hair, suggesting it wasn't the first time he'd done so this evening. 'I don't even want to think about my mother and sex in the same sentence.'

'You're being terribly old-fashioned, James,' Aiesha said. 'Your father's getting it on with any female under twenty-five with a pulse, and yet you won't allow your mother to be in a mature and respectable relationship? That's hardly fair.'

His forehead was still furrowed. 'I don't want to see her get hurt.'

'She's in love. Of course she'll get hurt.'

His gaze met hers. Held it steady. 'Have you ever been in love?'

Aiesha laughed. 'Are you joking? I'm not the falling-in-love type. I use men and spit them out once I'm done with them. Surely you know that much about me.'

'I know you don't like people getting close to you.' He was suddenly close enough for her to smell his cologne. Close enough to see the flare of his pupils. Close enough to feel the desire wafting off him like a hot summer breeze. It warmed her from head to foot. Burned her. Scorched her. 'I know you like to show everyone how tough you are, when on the inside you're anything but.'

Aiesha goaded him with her gaze. 'You want to get close to me, James? Then get your gear off and let's do it.'

He took her by the top of her shoulders and slowly but surely brought her flush against his body. 'I think my mother has some weird notion that we'll fall in love with each other.'

'She's dreaming.'

He brought his mouth down to the corner of hers, his lips barely touching her top lip. 'That's what I told her.'

Aiesha's insides shivered as his warm breath skated over her lips. 'It would never work. You're too traditional. Too straitlaced and proper.'

'And you're too wild and unpredictable.' He moved his mouth to her lower lip, pushing against it in soft little nudges that made her legs threaten to give way. 'Too uncontrollable.'

She pushed her lips against his, teasing him the way

he was teasing her. Tempting her. Torturing her. *Why don't you kiss me, damn it?* 'Control is your middle name, isn't it? James Control Challender. Got quite a ring to it, hasn't it?'

He smiled against the side of her mouth. 'I think you secretly like that about me.'

She put her hands against his neck, leaning into his erection. 'What? You think I *like* you?'

He brushed his lips against hers, not a kiss, not a caress, but something in between. 'You don't want to like me. You don't want to like anyone. My mother is the exception… Oh, and Bonnie, of course.'

Aiesha jerked her chin back against her chest. 'That overweight and incontinent hair machine?'

He cupped her left cheek with the broad span of his hand, his sapphire-blue eyes holding hers. 'There was a chewy treat on her bed when I brought her in from her last walk. I didn't put it there, so that only leaves you.'

She hadn't realised he would find it before Bonnie. She had tucked it in under the cushioned bed so Bonnie could sniff it out later. 'Your mother gave me instructions on how to take care of her dog. I'm only doing what I was told to do.'

He put his hands on her hips, bringing her close again. 'I told myself I wouldn't do this. I promised myself I wouldn't complicate things by getting involved with you.'

'It's just sex, James. People do it all the time. It doesn't have to mean anything.'

His eyes searched hers for a beat or two. 'I want you, but that must surely be obvious by now.'

Aiesha brought his head down so his mouth was within a breath of hers. 'Then for God's sake do something about it.'

He covered her mouth with his in a long and passionate kiss that fanned the flames already burning inside her. His lips were firm and gentle in turn, a tantalising mix of dominance and reverence that made her wonder why she had thought him so uptight and starchy. His tongue tangled with hers, taming it into submission, only to let her have free rein to do the same to him. Desire raced through her, heating her core, turning it to liquid as he took back control of the kiss. His tongue stabbed and thrust, rolled and dived, flicked and darted and then caressed and soothed. His hands moved from her hips to skim over her breasts, the touch so light and yet it made her flesh shiver and sing.

He made a deep, growly sound as he slid a hand under her sweater and found her lace-covered breast. He cupped her through the cobwebby fabric, rolling his thumb over her tight nipple, swallowing her gasp as he deepened his kiss.

Aiesha felt his hands move behind her back and unclip her bra. It fell to the floor as she raised her arms to haul off her sweater. His eyes drank in the sight of her, his hands moving over her in a caress that was possessive and yet worshipful.

'You're beautiful…so damn beautiful.' He bent his head and took her nipple in his mouth, sucking on her with such exquisite tenderness she felt every nerve in her body tremble in response. His tongue circled her nipple and then he moved to the underside of her breast, dragging his tongue along her flesh, making her mindless and breathless with want.

She *felt* beautiful when he touched her like that. Beautiful and desirable and feminine and...respected. There was nothing sleazy about his touch. He made her feel as if she was the only woman he ever wanted to make love with. The only one he wanted to share the intimate connection of body and soul.

He went to her other breast, exploring it in the same intimate detail, driving her senses into a wild frenzy as he subjected her to caress after caress, stroke after stroke, kiss after kiss. He moved back up to her neck, his lips playing with the sensitive skin there, lingering over her ear lobes and the delicate spot below.

He came back to her mouth, kissing her deeply and passionately while her lower body burned and ached for him with a need so strong it surpassed anything she had experienced before. She wasn't used to being swept away on a tumultuous tide of desire. She was used to being the one in control, mentally and physically always a step or two ahead. But his kiss and his touch had a magical effect on her senses, sending them spinning and twirling in rapturous delight.

She undid his belt and unzipped him, taking him in her hands to stroke and titillate. To explore him, to make him feel the uncontrollable desire she was feeling. He made deliciously male noises of heavy arousal, his erection thick and hard in her hand.

His hands went to the waistband of her yoga pants, ruthlessly tugging them down so they fell to her ankles. She stepped out of them and her knickers as he shucked

off his own trousers and underwear and shrugged off
his shirt.

Aiesha fed off the sight of him with a hunger she
had never felt with such intensity. He was lean and
yet muscled in all the right places. His abdomen was
washboard-flat, the pipelike ridges showcased beneath
the tanned olive-toned skin. His chest was lightly covered in hair that spread from his pectoral muscles, down
past his navel and to his groin, where his erection rose
proudly.

'On the floor.' It was a gruff command that thrilled
her as much as it surprised her. But she obeyed as
meekly as a submissive to a master.

He deftly dealt with the application of a condom
before he came down to join her. But he didn't rush to
penetrate her. Instead he gently eased her thighs apart
and brought his mouth to her intimately in a gentle caress that made her back arch in delight.

Aiesha had been pleasured that way before but she
had never been able to let herself fully relax enough to
orgasm. Her previous partners had performed the act
in a perfunctory manner, as if they had realised it was
what was expected but they didn't take the time to ask
her what she liked, or what worked and what didn't. It
had annoyed her that they thought they knew her body
better than she knew it herself so she had cut it short by
pretending to orgasm like a porn star, while privately
she'd mocked them for their ignorance and arrogance.

But this was different.

James stroked her with his tongue, but then stopped

to ask if it was too strong or too light. 'Tell me what you like best. Hard or soft? Fast or slow?'

Aiesha could barely speak for the sensations that were coursing through her. 'Just like that…slow and gradually building up… Oh, God…*ohhhhhh*.'

Her body gave a convulsing spasm, every nerve quivering and then exploding like fireworks. The rippling waves gradually died away, her body feeling as limp and pliable as melted wax.

She felt strangely unguarded, unexpectedly vulnerable. He had unlocked her senses in a way no one else had. Sex was supposed to be just sex. He had taken it to another level…one she had never visited before.

He came over her, one thigh draped over one of hers, his hand brushing her hair out of her face. 'You OK?'

Aiesha snapped out of her daze. 'Sure, why wouldn't I be?'

He studied her for a moment. 'We don't have to do this if you're having second thoughts.'

Second thoughts? Was he kidding? But how considerate of him not to assume he had the right to continue. It made another layer of her armour peel away. She put a hand to his face, stroking it over the dark, sexy stubble, her core contracting with another wave of longing. 'We can't let that condom go to waste, now can we?'

He took her hand in his and brought it up to his mouth, kissing each of her fingertips as his eyes held hers. 'I don't know about you, but I hate unnecessary waste.'

She put her hand around the back of his neck and pulled him down. 'Me, too.'

His mouth fused with hers in a smoking-hot kiss that made her belly quake all over again. His tongue got busy with hers, teasing and stroking and tangoing until she was making soft little whimpering sounds at the back of her throat.

He put a hand below her bottom and raised her to receive him, entering her in a long, slow, smooth glide that made her shiver all over in delight. Her body gripped him tightly, the friction of his first slow thrusts making her senses go crazy. He rocked gently at first, taking his time as he let her catch his rhythm, letting her get used to the breadth and length of him. Then he gradually picked up his pace, bringing her along with him, the excitement building all over again in her body. The tightening of her core, the swelling and throbbing ache of her clitoris, aching and pulsing for his touch.

He rolled her over so she was on top of him, his hand firm on her bottom as he kept his thrusts going. How did he know this was the only way she could orgasm without direct stimulation? She felt the first wave of pleasure like an explosion in her body. She arched her back and rode him in a desperate, wanton manner, her hair flying about her shoulders as she followed the tantalising lure of a mind-blowing orgasm.

And then she was there. Flying off into the stratosphere with a panting cry as the pleasure rocked through her like a powerful earthquake. She shook and shuddered, she whimpered and cried. She clung on as the last waves washed over her, leaving her floating in a place where no thought could spoil the glow of ultimate pleasure.

James rolled her back over to her back, still thickly, powerfully encased in her body, his eyes glittering with the build-up of passion. 'Good for you?'

Aiesha moved her body against him, wanting him to finally let go so she could feel the vibrations of his release. 'You know it was.'

The dark blue in his eyes darkened to a shade short of black. 'You could be pretending. It's hard for most men to tell the difference.'

She cocked her head at him. 'But I suppose you can?'

He brushed his lips against hers. 'Let's put it this way. I don't stop until I'm absolutely sure.'

Aiesha shivered again as he began to thrust deeply and rhythmically. His pace went from slow, almost lazily so, but then he gradually upped the speed until he was rocking against her, sending shockwaves of pleasure through her like thrashing waves against a cliff face.

She gripped the taut curve of his buttocks, holding him to her, urging him on, delighting in the weight of him, the way he filled her, stretched her, tantalised her with the friction of male desire against female flesh. She was climbing towards the summit again, all of her nerves tight as a tripwire, all the sensations gathering again in the tightly swollen bud of her clitoris.

She wanted to come so badly but wondered if she should tell him what she needed to get there. But then he repositioned himself, shifting slightly so he could bring his hand down to her, stroking her with just the right pressure and speed.

It was impossible not to come. She threw her head

back and succumbed to it, letting it rip through her like a speeding train. It shook and rattled her from head to foot until she was gasping and just shy of sobbing.

And *still* he hadn't taken his own pleasure.

Aiesha marvelled at his self-control but another part of her felt a tiny bit irritated by it. Did he find her so easy to resist? Wasn't he the *least* bit overcome by his passion for her by now? In her experience, men got her orgasm out of the way, often times in a token fashion, and went for their own with a single-minded and often selfish determination. They shifted her to the position they wanted and pumped away, not checking to see if she was too tender or uncomfortable.

But James waited until she was breathing normally again. He even stroked her hair back off her face, watching her with those ink-dark eyes. 'Ready for round three?'

'I only ever orgasm a couple of times, if that.' *Sometimes not at all.*

The corners of his mouth lifted. 'First time for everything.'

Aiesha's belly quivered at the smouldering look in his eyes. 'What about you?'

'I'm getting to that.'

She stifled a gasp as he started those slow but deliciously rhythmic thrusts. 'Are you counting backwards or thinking of your mother doing it or something?'

He stroked a lazy hand over the curve of her breast. 'What's the rush?'

She gave him an arch look. 'What's the hold-up?'

A slight frown pulled at his brow. 'Are you uncomfortable?'

'No, it's just I'm not used to a guy taking so long to get the job done. I'm used to "wham, bam, did you come? Thank you, ma'am."'

He studied her expression for a long beat or two. 'You don't always enjoy sex?'

Aiesha wished she hadn't been so transparent. 'I didn't say that.'

'You implied it.'

She concentrated her gaze at the V-shaped dish at the top of his sternum. Why did he persist in trying to *know* her? She didn't want to be known. She wanted to be separate. Unknowable. Unreachable. *Didn't she?* 'Sex is sex.'

He tipped up her chin with a fingertip, locking his gaze with hers. 'Sex can be so much more than that.'

Aiesha was conscious of the length of him still buried deep inside her. He had stilled his movements, but he was *there*. Waiting. Wanting. She tried to disguise a swallow but she saw his eyes follow the up and down motion of her throat. She sent the point of her tongue out in a quick brush over her lips, but he followed that, too. Then he traced the outline of her mouth with the tip of his index finger in an achingly slow motion, every millimetre of her flesh tingling at the contact. Nerves she didn't know she possessed hummed and buzzed. Her body trembled, the need building to a level she hadn't encountered before. Was this how it was supposed to feel? Wanting someone so much it physically hurt? Needing their touch so much it was as important and as necessary as the air she breathed? How could she have sold herself short for all this time?

His eyes came back to mesh with hers. 'Sex is all about the destination.' He began to move, deep and slow, each movement triggering another wave of thrilling pleasure through her body. 'Making love is about the journey, as well.' He kissed her mouth lightly, once, twice, but the third time was deep and lingering.

Aiesha lifted her hips, rolled her pelvis, teasing him with the slippery friction of her body. He increased his pace but he was still in control. She stroked his buttocks, and then dipped her fingers between them to the supersensitive skin of his perineum. He stifled a groan against her mouth and drove harder. She rode with him, urging him on with little gasps and whimpers as the need rose to a crescendo in her body. She could feel the tension in his muscles as he poised in that pivotal moment before the primal force took over. He gave another raw groan, his skin peppering with goose bumps beneath her fingertips like fine gravel as he shuddered and then flowed.

Aiesha held him in the quiet aftermath, which was another new thing for her. She was normally the first to disengage, to disentangle, to gather her clothes and move on.

But she didn't want to sever the connection between them. Couldn't sever it. Not yet. Her body felt... at peace. Satiated. Floating in a sea of contentment, she had never felt quite like this before. Something about his lovemaking spoke to her deep inside her soul. Touched her. Moved her. His respect, his consideration and concern for her pleasure made her feel valued, treasured. *Safe*. His breath was warm against the side of her neck, his chest rising and falling with hers, his legs in a sexy tangle with hers. She absently moved her hands over his back and shoulders, exploring each contour of muscle and bone, each knob of his vertebrae, the dish in his lower spine, and back up again to play with the closely cropped hair on his head.

'How's that carpet burn?' he said.

Aiesha smiled as she met his teasing gaze. 'Either the carpet is too good a quality or you weren't going hard enough.'

The glint in his eyes intensified. 'I can fix that,' he said, and swooped down and covered her mouth with his.

CHAPTER NINE

IN THE EARLY hours of the morning, James rolled over sleepily to reach for Aiesha beside him in his bed but instead his hand found a cool, empty space. He looked for a long moment at the indentation on her pillow where her head had lain beside his. The faint trace of her perfume lingered in the air, the same delicate but deliciously intoxicating fragrance he could smell on his skin.

He sat upright, listening for sounds of her moving about in the en-suite bathroom, but there was nothing but silence.

Empty silence.

He frowned as he pushed back the covers. He hadn't heard her leave. He hadn't expected her to leave. It made him feel like a gigolo who had served his purpose—a cheap hook-up that meant nothing to her. He didn't like the sense of being used. He had brought her upstairs because—all jokes aside—carpet burn wasn't his style, and he had a feeling it wasn't hers, either.

But then he remembered she'd told him she never spent the whole night with anyone. But surely *he* was different? He wasn't some nameless one-night stand she would never see again. He had taken the time to listen to her, to try and get to know her, to understand what put those shadows in her eyes.

He had *made love* to her.

He had taken the time to get to know her body as intimately as he could. She had responded to him with captivating fervour. Surely what they had shared meant more to her than a quick satiation of physical need?

He glanced at the bedside-table clock. It was 4:00 a.m. He shrugged on his bathrobe, telling himself he was only checking on her to see if she was all right.

Her bedroom was empty.

The bed had been slept in, or at least she had been in there because the sheets were all tangled and thrown back, the feather pillows crushed and misshapen. But whether she had slept or not was open to question.

How long had this restless bed-hopping been going on? When had it started? Why wouldn't she talk to him about it? If only he had realised at the outset how complex and traumatised she was he might have been able to get her to confide in him without all the game playing she went on with all the time. He still cringed at the way he had confronted her in the kitchen, accusing her of stealing. He had pushed her into a meltdown and in doing so he had lost his chance to earn her trust. How long would it take to win it back? Or was he fighting an unwinnable battle?

When he turned on the light in the kitchen Bonnie raised her head and blinked at him but didn't move from her cushioned bed near the cooker. She put her head back down on her paws and closed her eyes as she gave a deep doggy sigh.

James scanned the kitchen with his gaze. The kettle was stone-cold and there were no crumbs or used plates or discarded apple cores or milk cartons. He turned off the light and went further along the passage to the ballroom. The door was open enough for the moonlight to spill along the floor in a long silver beam.

The piano was a dark hulk in front of the windows, and beside it stood Aiesha with her back to the room, dressed in a silky ivory-coloured wrap that gave her the appearance of a ghost.

Knowing all too well the danger of sneaking up on her, James rapped his knuckles lightly against the door. 'Aiesha?'

She must have known he was there even before he knocked for there was nothing hurried or startled about her movements as she turned to look at him. It was difficult to read her expression, but with the moonlight silhouetting her slim body from behind he could see she was completely naked beneath the wrap.

'What are you doing down here all by yourself?' he said.

'Couldn't sleep.'

'Why didn't you wake me?'

She stepped out of the shadows, her eyebrows drawn together and her voice sharp with an edge of irritation to it. 'To do what? Make me a milky drink? Tell me a bedtime story?' She curled her lip and added in a mutter, 'Like that's ever happened before.'

James frowned. 'Sweetheart, what's going on?'

Her brows shot up mockingly. '*Sweetheart?* Isn't that taking this crazy charade a little too far?'

He came over to where she was standing so stiffly, so guardedly. 'What's the matter?'

A mask slipped down over her features. 'Nothing.'

'OK…so help me out here,' he said. 'Last time I looked, you were curled up in my arms and drifting off to sleep. Now it looks like you want to punch my lights out. Can you fill in the bits I've missed?'

Her eyes had that hard, streetwise sheen to them. 'Look, I don't mind sleeping with you, but I'm not sleeping with you, OK?'

'Want to run that by me one more time?'

'I'm not sharing a bed with you. It's too…intimate.'

James gave a wry laugh. 'And what we did a couple of hours ago wasn't?'

Two spots of colour rose high on her cheekbones. 'It was just sex.'

'What is it about being intimate that you find so terrifying?'

A frown of irritation puckered her forehead as she glared at him again. 'Why are you asking me these stupid questions?'

'I want to understand you.'

'And here I was thinking you only wanted me for my body.'

'I imagine most men do, but I like to think I'm a little less shallow than that.'

Her chin came up. Her eyes glinted. Challenging him. 'Well, guess what, *sweetheart*? My body is all that's on offer. Take it or leave it.'

James wanted to call her bluff. His mind told him to walk away. But his body craved her. Ached for her. Throbbed with a bone-deep longing that had not been assuaged by sleeping with her. Instead it fed his craving of her like an addict taking a hit. Desire was something he controlled, channelled.

But not with her.

He couldn't control it. He couldn't redirect it or tame it. It roared in his blood with the force of a tornado. 'Come here.'

Her chin went higher, those smoky grey eyes glittering with sensual heat. 'Why don't you come here?'

His groin pulsed with anticipation. 'I asked first.'

She tossed her hair back over her shoulders, the movement loosening her wrap so it revealed half of her left breast. 'You didn't ask,' she said. 'You commanded.'

'So?'

'So ask nicely.'

James was so hard he seriously wondered if he could even take a step. 'You want me to beg?'

Her lips curved upwards in a sexy half smile as she sauntered over to him, her wrap falling away from her to land in a puddle of silk on the floor. 'Would you?'

'I think you know me better than that.'

He sucked in a breath as she trailed a fingertip down the open V of his bathrobe. She got to his navel, circling it ever so slowly, her eyes locked on his. 'Want me to go lower?' she asked.

'How low are you prepared to go?'

Her naughty-girl smile made his insides quake with lust. Her touch was like a spreading fire. His heart pounded with excitement as she slithered down his body to drop to her knees in front of him. 'This low enough for you?' Her warm breath danced over his rigid flesh. Teasing him. Torturing him with the promise of her erotic possession.

He was swaying on his feet, struggling to keep himself steady as her mouth hovered so tantalisingly close. 'Wait. I need to get a condom.' He fished in his bathrobe pocket and handed it to her. 'Want to do the honours?'

Her eyes glinted. 'With pleasure.'

James held his breath as she ripped the foil packet with her teeth, spitting the piece to one side, before taking the condom in her hand and rolling it down the length of him. Her fingers smoothed it into place, driving him wild with each stroke and glide of her hand.

She moved in closer, breathing over him again, ramping up his anticipation, and escalating his excitement to fever pitch. Her tongue touched him, a tiny stab of a touch that even through the layer of latex was electric. She touched him again, a stroking caress that travelled the length of him, from swollen head to thickened base. Every hair on his scalp stood up. The backs of his knees tingled. The base of his spine fizzed.

Her tongue came back up, circled the top of him before taking him into her warm, wet mouth. He groaned as she sucked on him, slowly at first, but then she increased the pressure and suction until he was in danger of spinning out of control.

He gripped her by the head, his fingers clutching at handfuls of her hair, but she refused to relinquish her hold on him. She brought him to the brink and then ruthlessly pushed him over. He lost himself in the moment of climax, the waves of intense pleasure rippling through his groin as he surged, pulsed, shuddered. Emptied.

She gave him a smouldering smile as she crawled back up his body, her naked breasts brushing against his chest, her pelvis warm and tempting as it rubbed against him. She was every erotic fantasy he'd ever had: sultry, sinful and playfully slutty, and yet sensitive and sensual. 'Want to go another round?' she said.

James threaded his hands through her tousled hair. 'I need another condom first.'

She slid her hands over his pectoral muscles. 'I don't suppose you have another one conveniently placed in your bathrobe pocket?'

'Sadly, no.'

Her eyes brightened mischievously. 'Well, this is your lucky day because I've got one in mine.'

James watched as she walked over to the puddle of her silky wrap lying on the floor and retrieved a condom. Every one of her movements tantalised him. Made him hard. The way she bent down, giving him a full view of those long slender legs and that gorgeously neat bottom. The way she came back over to him with her pert breasts with their rosy nipples on glorious show. Her body was a temple of temptation. Long-limbed and slim, curved and toned, her head glossy and sexily tousled, her mouth shiny and moist. Every cell in his body responded to the sight of her. Throbbed and ached to be joined with her.

She did a repeat performance of tearing the packet

with her teeth, taking her time to roll it over him, holding his gaze in a scorching lock that made his body throb and burn anew with lust.

He took her by the shoulders and tugged her towards him, crushing her mouth beneath his in a fiery kiss. Her mouth opened under his, taking him in, devouring him. Her kiss was hot and urgent, as hot and urgent and desperate as his.

His hands moved over her body, her breasts, her hips, her feminine folds, touching, teasing, promising more but not giving it until she was making throaty little pleas. He was as ruthless with her as she had been with him. Ramping up her desire, making her beg for the release she craved.

'Now, oh, for God's sake, *now*,' she said against his mouth.

'Not yet.' He softly bit her lower lip. 'Don't be so impatient.'

She bit him back, harder, making his knees buckle. 'I want you inside me.'

He walked her, thigh to thigh, to the nearest wall, his mouth working its way around hers in teasing little nips and nudges. 'What's the big hurry?'

She clutched at his buttocks, pulling him closer. He could smell her salty and musky fragrance, the alluring heat of feminine arousal that made his need of her all the more overwhelming. He slipped a finger inside her, applying the lightest friction to her swollen need, swallowing her gasp as he captured her mouth beneath his. Her tongue moved with his in a combative dance, an exciting fast-paced tango of lust and longing and battle for control.

Holding her in his arms was like holding a powder keg and a match. She was the most exciting, thrilling lover he had ever had. He had never wanted someone as much as he wanted her. It was a driving need that dominated every waking moment. It was like being under a spell, a magical, sensual spell that was inescapable. Her flirtatious behaviour infuriated and inflamed him in equal measure. She was everything he avoided in a partner and yet she was everything he found so breathtakingly exciting.

She grabbed at his hair, her mouth breathing hot sexy fumes of lust into his. 'I want you. *Now*.'

James turned her so her back was against him, her hands splayed on the wall in front of her. He didn't have to nudge her thighs apart. She had already anticipated his intention. She gave a sexy little groan and wriggled her bottom against his erection, goading him on. It was an invitation he could not resist. He entered her in a deep, slick thrust, pleasure shooting through him like an electrifying pulse as her tight little body gripped him. He rocked against her, breathing in the fragrance of her hair that was brushing against his face. She made panting little noises, gasping noises, whimpering-with-pleasure noises, which made him drive all the harder and faster.

He gripped her by the hips, clenching his jaw to keep himself from coming too soon. She rose up on tiptoe, searching for more direct friction. He brought his hand around to stroke her with his fingers, the swollen nub slick and damp with moisture. He felt the contractions of her orgasm, each powerful spasm in time with her cries of ecstasy.

He drove himself over the edge, breathing hard, flying high in a whirlpool of sensations that made his body shudder all over with reaction.

He kept her pinned to the wall even though his erection was subsiding. Her hair tickled his cheek; the scent of her teased his nostrils. He lifted her hair out of the way and kissed the back of her neck in a series of soft-as-air kisses, delighting in the way she shivered under his touch. 'You like that?' he asked.

'Mmm…' She gave a dreamy-sounding sigh.

He kissed the cup of her shoulder, using his tongue to tease her soft skin. She made another purring sound of pleasure as he worked his way up the side of her neck, lingering at the spot just below her ear. He wondered if she was as responsive with other men. The thought was jarring. The image of her with other lovers stirred an uneasy feeling in his stomach. Jealousy wasn't something he had felt before. None of his partners had given him any reason to be jealous. He knew they'd had previous lovers; it was unfair in this day and age to expect anything else.

How many men had Aiesha been with?

Did it matter?

James stepped back and dealt with the condom, trying to get his double standard back in the Dark Ages where it belonged. It was none of his business how much experience she had. It wasn't as if their relationship was going to continue beyond a couple of weeks. How could it? She resented the world he came from. She didn't even *like* him. She saw him as a trophy to collect, a prize to show off. A box to tick. She might enjoy having sex with him, but that was all she wanted from him.

And it was all he wanted from her...*wasn't it*?

She picked up her wrap from the floor and slipped it over her shoulders, her grey gaze connecting with his. 'There haven't been as many as you think.'

James tied his own robe before he answered. 'How many what?'

'Men. Lovers.' She tied the ribbons of her wrap around her waist. 'The press make me seem like a tart. But it's not like I'm out there every night getting it on with someone. You're my first this year.'

He gave her a look. 'Not bad considering it's the tenth of January.'

Her lips tilted in a little smile. 'You hungry?'

'Are we talking about breakfast?'

She sashayed over to him, running her fingertips down the length of his forearm. 'Are you an early riser?'

James was rising now and she only had to move an inch closer to feel it. 'When I need to be. What about you?'

That smouldering look was back in her eyes, making his spine tingle at the base. 'Oh, I'm *very* flexible.' She untied his bathrobe and slid her hand down his abdomen in a slow caress. 'I take each day as it comes.'

He sucked in a breath as she took hold of him. The glint in her eyes drove him wild. Everything about her drove him wild. The way she ran the tip of her tongue over her lush mouth nearly sent him over the edge. Her sexily tousled hair tickled his chest as she pressed herself close. Her slender hips rubbed against his pelvis, inciting him, arousing him all over again. He placed his hands on her bottom and brought her even closer. 'Just as well this snow is on the melt because at this rate I'm going to run out of condoms,' he said.

She trailed a fingertip along his stubbled jaw and then over his lower lip, making every nerve twitch and dance. 'In future you'll know to be better prepared then, won't you?'

In future...

What future?

This couldn't go on for ever. How could it? Aiesha didn't develop bonds with people, not unless they served her interests. How could he be sure she wanted to be with him, other than for the prestige and protection his name and money provided? It would always play at the back of his mind. Did she care about *him* or what he could give her?

James slid his hands up her arms to hold her by the shoulders. 'You do realise this thing we have going isn't going to continue beyond the end of the month, don't you?'

Her mouth curved upwards, her grey eyes glinting mockingly. 'But of course. You're paying me to play a role.' Her fingers tiptoed up his chest. 'Am I giving good service so far?'

He dropped his hands and stepped away from her. 'Don't.'

'Don't what?' Her look was all beguiling innocence. 'Say it as it is? Come on, James. Don't be such a prude.

I'm your paid mistress. Don't all rich posh guys have one? Your father certainly does. She even looks a bit like me, don't you think?'

James clenched his jaw. He knew she was deliberately baiting him. It was her favourite pastime. But it annoyed him that she seemed not to be the least worried or conflicted by their situation. She wanted him and she'd got him. The trap had been set on day one and, like a fool, he had stepped into it. Now she was playing the hired hooker to make him squirm with guilt. She was well aware of how much he hated the thought of being compared to his father, of being tarred with the same cheap, dirty little brush. She was well aware of it and was maximising it for...for what? More money? Revenge? Just for the sheer heck of it? Didn't her behaviour prove how little she cared for him as a person? She was in it for what she could get and was shamelessly brazen about it.

'You are currently my fiancée,' he said. 'That's what the press thinks and I want them to continue to think it until such time as I inform them otherwise. Understood?'

She gave him a mercurial smile. 'Then you'd better get a wriggle on and buy me a big, expensive ring or no one will believe you.'

James muttered an expletive under his breath. 'Be ready by lunchtime. If we can't drive out I'll hire a helicopter to fly us out.'

CHAPTER TEN

AIESHA DECIDED JAMES'S anger was a good thing. He kept his distance on the trip over to Paris, barely speaking a word to her, keeping himself busy with his laptop, as if they were two strangers travelling together. But that was fine by her as she needed time to regroup. It was becoming confusing to be playing one role while feeling something else. *Feeling* was something she wasn't used to doing. Feeling was dangerous. Attachment was dangerous. *Bonding* was dangerous. She could be physical with someone without emotional engagement.

Of course she could.

Men did it all the time. Sex was a physical need like any other. She was not going to be stupid and fall in love. Not with James. Not with the one man who would never love her back. Why would he? She had all but destroyed his precious family. She knew he wasn't close to his father, but a relationship with her was only going to make his relationship with him so much worse.

His mother, Louise, might accept her but even that was stretching a dream way too far. The world Aiesha came from was so disparate, so foreign, so totally alien it was as if she had come from another universe. How could the chasm ever be breached? Everyone would look down on her, watching for her to make a slip-up. To say something she shouldn't say. To wear something not quite appropriate. To bring more shame and disgrace on the Challender name.

It was stupid to think of a future with James. He would never allow himself to love someone so unsuitable. She was a lounge singer from Sin City. Fairy-tale endings didn't happen to girls like her.

And the sooner she accepted it the better.

The press didn't show up until they arrived at the boutique hotel, a short walking distance from the Eiffel Tower. James took Aiesha's hand and led her through the foyer, answering in fluent French the barrage of questions from the crush of journalists and photographers. From her limited grasp of the language, Aiesha was able to pick up one or two phrases that communicated James's delight at their engagement and how he was looking forward to their wedding at some point during the year. He even managed to get her to the private lift to the penthouse floor without losing his urbane smile.

But once the doors closed he dropped his arm from around her waist and let out a stiff curse. 'This is ridiculous. How long are they going to hound us like this? It's not as if we're celebrities. Why are they so interested in us?'

Aiesha leaned against the waist-height brass rail on the wall of the lift. 'You're rich. You're handsome. People want to know what you're doing and who you're doing it with.'

He pushed a hand through his hair, his frown formidably dark. Aiesha knew he hated all the press attention because it made him appear like his father, holing up in a hotel with his latest lover. James was so private about his life it would torture him to have his every move anticipated and speculated and commented on. Her presence in his life was only intensifying that speculation. Was that why he was so brooding and prickly now they were back in the spotlight? At Lochbannon he could temporarily forget about the rest of the world, but now the world was after him for an exclusive on his engagement and wedding plans. No wonder he was looking antsy and conflicted. Which made her all the more determined to show she wasn't…even though she was. Desperately.

'I've organised an outfit for you to wear for the dinner tomorrow night and one for this evening,' he said into the silence. 'I've also arranged for a jeweller to bring some samples of rings to our room.' He pushed his sleeve back to glance at his watch with a preoccupied frown. 'He should be here in a couple of hours.'

'So…' Aiesha sent him a little smile. 'What will we do in the meantime?'

His mouth was pinched tight, although she could see the way his gaze slipped to the swell of her breasts and back again. 'Do you ever think of anything else but sex?'

She gave him an arch look. 'That's what you're paying me for, isn't it?'

He snatched her wrist as the lift doors pinged open, marching her out like a captor with a prisoner. 'I'm a little tired of you making those cheap little digs. We wouldn't be in this situation if you hadn't sent that first tweet, remember?' He jerked his head to indicate for her to enter the penthouse.

'Aren't you going to carry me over the threshold?'

'Get inside.'

She raised her chin. 'I want my own room.'

'I want you with me.'

'What if I don't want to be with you?'

A nerve twitched in his jaw, his eyes blue-black. 'This is your room. In here. With me. End of discussion.'

Aiesha fought her agitation by redirecting it into anger. She stabbed a finger at his chest, leaning her whole weight into it, but even so he didn't move a millimetre. She felt like a wispy blade of grass trying to push over a tree trunk. 'You do *not* tell me where I will sleep. Get it?'

He plucked her hand off his chest, holding it so firmly her fingers overlapped each other. He tugged her against him, his eyes holding hers in a tense little lock. 'I know what you're up to, Aiesha. You want me to lose my head. To lose my temper and act like a moron, like you believe all men to be. But it won't work. Push and defy me all you want. I'm not going to let you win. You will stay with me all night, no matter what.'

He stepped back from her, his expression enviably cool and controlled. 'I'm going to meet with my client. By the time I get back, the jeweller and the clothes will be here. Don't leave the hotel until I get back. The press are still out there.'

Aiesha threw him a mutinous glare. 'You can't tell me what to do.'

He opened the door, pausing to look back at her before he left. 'I just did.'

Aiesha waited until she saw James leave the front of the hotel in a cab before she picked up her coat and purse. She was not having him tell her what she could or couldn't do. She needed fresh air and she was going to go out and get some. He had no right to order her about as if she had no will of her own.

No man had that right.

She slipped out of a side door and managed to escape the attention of the press because a minor member of European royalty arrived and the cameras switched their focus on them instead.

The streets were slippery and icy from melting snow and a breeze that felt as if it had icicles attached sharpened the air. She put her head down against the cold and walked at a brisk pace to get warm. Paris was beautiful, no matter what the season, but with the Eiffel Tower and every building and bridge and cathedral spire painted white with snow it was particularly picturesque, giving it an old-world, timeless feel.

Aiesha walked along the banks of the Seine, where conical pines stood like powdered sentries along the whitened pathway. The park benches lined along the walk were encrusted with virgin snow, for no one had sat down and lingered there to take in the view due to the bitter cold.

She walked for over an hour and then began to retrace her steps and was only a few blocks from the hotel when she saw it happen. A man wearing a thick dark coat was dragging a small dog behind him on a lead. The little mutt didn't seem too happy on being pulled along and was wriggling and shaking its head from side to side to try and escape. The man said something foul in French and dragged the dog into a nearby alley.

Aiesha's blood ran as cold as the ice beneath her feet. Her heart started to thump so loudly she could hear it in her ears. Her stomach churned and, in spite of the freezing conditions, sweat broke out on her brow. Her legs felt as if they were stuck in the pavement, her ankles held there by steel vices.

But then she heard the little dog yelp and she was galvanised like a sprinter leaping off the block when the starter gun was fired. '*No!*' She ran screaming into the alley, slipping and sliding all over the place like a newborn foal on ice skates. She fell painfully to her knees and scrambled back up, her heart beating so frantically she could barely speak. 'No, please don't hurt him. Please don't hurt him.'

The man looked at her as if she were a crazed idiot. Even the little dog took one look at her and cowered behind its owner's legs. 'You are crazy, *oui*?' the man said.

Aiesha put her hand out for the dog's lead. 'Give me the dog.'

The man scooped the dog up and held it underneath his right arm, glaring at her. 'Get away from me.'

She took out her purse with hands that were shaking so badly several coins fell out as she opened it. 'Look, I'll pay you. Here, take this. It's all I've got on me. Let me have the dog. *Please*, let me have the dog.'

The man screwed up his face. 'You are mad. It is not even a pedigree dog. It's twelve years old and has teeth missing.'

Aiesha was shivering and sick and her head was pounding so badly she felt spaced out and light-headed. It was as if she were looking down at herself from above. It was someone else down in the alleyway begging and pleading with the man to hand over his dog.

But then another person appeared in the alley, his voice so familiar as he called out her name she stumbled towards him, sobbing hysterically. 'James, quick. You have to do something.'

'What on earth's going on?' James gathered her in his arms, opening his coat to wrap her inside it against the strong wall of his chest. 'Hush now. It's all right. I'm here.'

'He's going to hurt it.' She clutched at his shirt lapels in desperation. 'You have to stop him. He's going to kill it.'

'That lady is crazy!' the man said. 'She tried to steal my wife's dog, then she tried to buy it off me.'

James kept one hand on the back of Aiesha's head while he spoke to the man in French. 'My fiancée seems concerned you were going to harm the dog.'

'It's my wife's dog,' the man said. 'She's sick in bed so I offered to take the dog out. He doesn't like walking on the lead. But if I let him off he runs away from me and then I will be the one killed, *oui*?'

Aiesha looked up at James. 'What's he saying?'

'I'll explain later.' He turned to the man. 'I'm sorry for the misunderstanding. I hope your wife gets better soon.'

The man shifted his bulky body inside his coat like a bantam rooster after a fight with a rival who had outmatched him. He patted the dog, who subsequently licked his hand and looked up at him with bright button eyes. 'Come on, Babou,' the man said. 'Didn't I always tell you the English are mad?'

Aiesha bit her lip as she watched the man open a door further down the alley leading to a block of flats. 'I guess that's where he lives…'

'Yes, with his wife.' James looked down at her with a concerned expression. 'Are you OK?'

'I'm fine.'

'No, you're not. You're shaking.'

'Can we go back to the hotel?' She gave a long shuddery sigh. 'I'm cold and wet and…and I need a drink.'

He took her hand and led her out of the alley. 'I think I could do with one, too.'

James kept his arm around her on the way back to their hotel. She was still shivering and shaking but he wanted to get her warm and safe before he pressed her about the incident with the dog. He had thought her little tantrum the other night was bad but this was so much worse. He had never seen her so hysterical. So emotionally undone. At first he'd thought she was in danger. Seeing her in that alleyway confronting an angry-looking man had given him a visceral blow to his heart. The thought of her being attacked or harmed in any way had been like a knockout punch to his solar plexus. He tried to convince himself he would be just as concerned for a stranger but he knew it wasn't true. It physically *hurt* to see her in danger. His chest still felt tight, restricted. Painful.

He wondered what was behind her reaction. She didn't even like dogs…or so she said. What was she doing trying to rescue one that didn't even need rescuing? Did it have something to do with her past? Would she tell him if he asked or would she give him that hard, steely look and tell him to mind his own business? He could only push her so far. He had learnt that the hard way. When would she finally let him in? He wanted to know what put those dark shadows in her eyes. He wanted to know what gave her that sharp tongue and don't-mess-with-me air. He wanted to know what had made her so prickly and defensive that she pushed away anyone who showed the least bit of care for her.

'How did you know where I was?' she asked when they got back to their suite.

James took her coat off her. 'I was in a cab on my way back to the hotel and I saw you run into the alley. At first I thought you were trying to hide from me. I paid off the cab and got to you just as you were about to floor that poor man. What was that all about? I thought you didn't like dogs?'

She peeled off her scarf without meeting his gaze. 'I don't like seeing dogs mistreated. I thought he was being unkind to it. I overreacted. I'm sorry. My mistake. Can we forget about it now?'

'No, Aiesha,' he said. 'I want to know why you were so upset. Talk to me. Tell me why you got so hysterical.'

At first he thought she was going to refuse. She was rolling her scarf around one of her hands, the action mechanical, automated as if her mind was elsewhere. But then he saw the moment the screen came down. It was like watching a suit of armour being removed piece by piece. It started with her eyes, moved down to her mouth, her neck, and her shoulders—her whole body finally losing its tightly held stance.

'I should've known...' she said in a voice that vibrated with self-recrimination. 'I should've known he would kill Archie to get back at me.'

James's stomach plummeted and his heart lurched as if someone had shoved it. He swallowed thickly. 'Who was Archie?'

The sadness in her grey eyes was overwhelming. 'My dog.'

He was connecting the dots but it was a horrible picture that was forming in his mind. A ghastly scenario that he could see reflected in her pain-filled gaze. 'Your stepfather?'

'Yes...'

James gathered her close, his head resting on the top of her head as he tried to absorb some of her pain. 'Oh, you poor little baby,' he said in a shocked whisper.

She wrapped her arms around his waist and leaned against him as if he was the only thing she could rely on to keep her upright. She spoke in a muffled tone against his chest, telling him things he wished he didn't have to hear, but he knew how cathartic this moment was for her. She was finally letting him in. Revealing everything about her past. About her pain. Why she was the way she was. He thought of her as that terrified young teenager, traumatised beyond belief and yet hiding it behind a mask of come-close-to-me-at-your-peril. His mother had seen through it eventually, but it shamed him that it had taken him so long.

He continued to stroke her silky head, letting her speak of the unspeakable, letting her release the pent-up anger and rage that had festered inside her for so long.

Then there was silence.

James was loath to break it but he could feel her shivering from cold and reaction. He eased back to look at her face, ravaged by grief and anger and tears that had taken a decade to spill from her eyes. He was so glad she had chosen to tell him. So relieved. So honoured. It made him feel as if she finally saw him as someone she could trust. Not someone who would exploit her or betray her. It was a nice feeling. A good feeling. He blotted her wet cheeks with the pad of his thumb. 'Let's get you into a nice hot bath. I'll tell the jeweller to push back our appointment an hour.'

She put her hand over his and held it to her cheek. 'James…'

He looked into her tear-washed grey eyes. 'Yes?'

She chewed at her lip, looking so young and vulnerable his chest cramped. 'I've never told anyone that… Not even your mother.'

He brushed a wisp of hair off her forehead with a

gentle hand. 'I wish I'd known ten years ago. I would've tried to help you.'

She trained her gaze on his shirt button. 'I'm sorry about that thing with your father... I never intended to do anything other than show your mother what a jerk he was. I didn't realise how much it would impact you.'

James tipped up her face to look into her eyes. 'I knew my parents were unhappy. If you hadn't brought things to a head, my mother might have struggled on in silence for God knows how long. I guess you can tell she's not the type to give up easily.'

She gave a long sigh. 'I owe her a lot. And how do I repay her? By stuffing up your engagement to Phoebe what's-her-name.'

James was a little shocked to realise he hadn't thought about Phoebe for days. He struggled to think of what he had liked about her. *Liked?* Wasn't he supposed to have loved her? *Had* he loved her? He had liked that Phoebe fitted in with his lifestyle, that she was poised and well spoken, well read and cultured. That she understood the demands of his career and was content to stay in the background and support him.

But there were things he hadn't liked, annoying little things he had chosen to ignore. Phoebe was not adventurous or playful, in bed or out of it. She was even more staid and formal than he was. She had no interest in people outside her social circle. She didn't stop to talk to the housekeeper or the gardener.

And she would definitely not run screaming down a Paris alley putting her own life in danger to rescue a little dog....

He gave himself a mental shake. 'Phoebe is probably dating her childhood sweetheart, Daniel Barnwell, as we speak.'

Aiesha frowned. 'Doesn't that upset you? That she moved on so quickly?'

James was pleasantly surprised it didn't upset him. Not as much as it should have. 'They'd been dating for years. They'd only broken up a couple of months before I came on the scene.'

She gave him a wry look. 'Seems I did you a big, fat favour then.'

He searched her features for a beat, wondering if she felt anything of the confusion he was currently feeling. Their relationship was a complex mix of reality and pretence. It felt real when he held her, kissed her, made love to her.

She was a complex mix of reality and pretence.

For years she had been the enemy. She seemed to relish the role, maximising any opportunity to score points against him. She mocked him, laughed at him and goaded him. How much of that was real and how much of it was a defence mechanism? Was she hiding a sweet and sensitive soul behind that brash in-your-face attitude? Or was she too damaged and hardened from the past? What did she think of him, *really* think of him? Did she care anything for him or was she using him like she used everyone else?

'What will you do when our relationship comes to an end?' he asked.

She gave a little shrug of one shoulder. 'Find a new job. Not in Vegas. Maybe on a cruise ship or something.

I might meet someone filthy rich who'll set me up for life. An old guy who'll cark it after a few months and leave me all his money.' She gave him a slanted smile. 'How cool would that be?'

James locked his jaw. She was at it again. Deliberately pressing his buttons. Game playing. Making him believe she was something she wasn't. He could see through it now. It was all an act. A charade. 'You don't mean that.'

She walked towards the bathroom with her hip-swinging gait. 'Sure I do.'

'I don't believe you,' he said. 'You want everyone to think the worst of you because deep down you believe you deserve it. But that's not who you are, Aiesha. You're not the bad girl everyone thinks you are. My mother saw through it. *I* can see through it. Don't insult me by pretending to be something you're not.'

Her look was all glittering defiance and her tilted smile all worldly mockery as she stood framed by the bathroom door. 'You're a fine one to talk. I might have sent the first tweet but you're the one who took it a step further by setting up this pretend engagement. At least I have the honesty to call it by its real name. It's a dirty little fling. A smutty little hook-up.' Her eyes glinted some more. 'And you're loving every filthy minute of it.'

James flinched as she closed the bathroom door with a resounding click.

She was right. God help him.

He was.

CHAPTER ELEVEN

WHEN AIESHA CAME out of the bathroom there was no sign of James. But laid out on the king-size bed was a collection of clothes—a midnight-blue velvet cocktail dress and a gorgeous evening gown in black satin with spaghetti-thin straps and long black gloves with a white, fluffy stole. There were shoes and an evening purse and a velvet-lined jewellery tray with a collection of diamond rings. She chose the simplest one, a princess-cut diamond that winked at her as she slipped it on her finger.

A sharp little pain gripped her deep inside her chest. This was another part of the charade. The fancy props that turned her into Cinderella for the ball. She dressed in the velvet cocktail dress, swept her hair up on her head, did her make-up, put on the shoes. Turned in front of the mirror to see how the dress showed off her long legs and trim figure. She wasn't vain but she knew she looked good. Glamorous and elegant. Polished.

But underneath all the finery she was still a girl from the wrong suburb. With the wrong accent. With the wrong relatives.

She was wrong.

The door of the suite opened and James stood there dressed in a dark grey suit with a white shirt and red and silver tie. Her breath caught. Her heart jumped. Had he ever looked more magnificent? So tall. So sophisticated. So breathtakingly, heart-stoppingly handsome.

'You look—' he seemed momentarily lost for words '—absolutely gorgeous.'

Aiesha smoothed her hands over her hips. 'I hope you don't expect me to eat anything. And you'd better hope and pray I don't cough or sneeze because I don't think this zip will be up to it.'

'Did you choose a ring?'

She held her left hand out for him to inspect. 'Yep.'

He glanced at the ring before his eyes met hers. Penetrated hers. 'You didn't like the others?'

'Nope.'

'But it's the cheapest one.'

Aiesha held it up to the light, watching as the facets of the diamond glittered. 'Doesn't look cheap to me.'

'It's not, but—'

'Don't worry, James.' She flashed him a quick little smile. 'I'll give it back when this is over. You can give it to your real bride.'

He stood looking down at her for a long moment, his brow creased in a frown.

'Have I got lipstick on my teeth or something?'

'No.'

'Then why are you looking at me like that?'

He moved his thumb over the back of her hand in a rhythmic motion, his eyes still holding hers. 'I thought we could go somewhere for a quiet drink. I know a cosy little bar where the music doesn't thrash your ears. You can actually have a conversation without having to shout or mime.'

He wanted to talk to her? That could be dangerous. She had said enough. She had already told him too much. He *knew* too much. 'Won't I look a little over-dressed?'

'This is Paris,' he said. 'It's impossible to be over-dressed.'

The bar he took her to was in Saint-Germain-des-Prés, where a pianist was playing blues and jazz. The atmosphere was warm and intimate and, although the drinks were crazily overpriced, Aiesha indulged in a brightly coloured cocktail that made her head spin after two sips. Or maybe it was being in James's company. He wasn't so stiff and formal and brooding now. He was watching her fiddle with her straw with an indulgent smile kicking up one side of his mouth as if he had solved a diffi-cult puzzle and was feeling rather pleased with himself.

She could only assume *she* was the puzzle.

He had been patient; she had to give him that. Wait-ing for her to drop her guard. Not pushing her too hard. And yet he had stood his ground with her on occasion, not letting her get away with manipulating him. 'Game playing' he called it. He was right. She did play games. It was her way of keeping people at a safe distance.

But she hadn't been able to keep him away from her secrets. He had discovered almost everything about her and yet he didn't push her away...or at least not until the end of the month when they would go their separate ways.

He would move on with his life and find a suitable bride. He would find someone who wouldn't play games. Someone he would be comfortable introducing to his friends and colleagues. Not someone who had the potential to embarrass him or destroy his reputation via an ill-timed comment to the press from one of her crazy relatives.

Why did it have to be this way? Why couldn't she be the one he chose? Why couldn't she accept him if he did?

Because that was the stuff of fairy tales and she wasn't a little kid any more, hoping that someone was going to wave a magic wand over her head and make everything turn out right in the end.

'I wouldn't drink that too quickly,' he said.

Aiesha gave her straw a couple of twirls before she took another sip. 'Don't worry, James. I won't embarrass you by suddenly jumping up and dancing on the tables.'

His smile was exchanged for a frown. 'Look, can you drop the armour just for tonight?'

Aiesha crossed one leg over the other and leaned back on the velvet sofa they were sharing. 'What armour?'

His dark blue eyes held hers. 'Let me see you without the brash bad-girl mask. Be the girl in the alley this afternoon. The one who loves dogs. The one who let me hold her as she told me stuff she's told no one before.'

She pursed her lips and reached for her drink, taking a generous sip that sent her blood-alcohol level soaring.

Or maybe it wasn't the alcohol. Maybe it was the chance to let her guard down and stay down long enough to connect with someone who was smart enough, intuitive enough to see behind the facade.

It was *so* tempting…

Could she do it?

Just for tonight?

What did she have to lose? It wasn't as if she had anything to lose or gain. James wasn't going to suddenly fall in love with her just because she showed him the side of herself no one ever saw. He cared about her, but then, so did his mother. It didn't mean he loved her or wanted to spend his future with her. He was too conservative, too sensible to fall for someone so far outside his social circle.

Aiesha kept her gaze trained on the pink-and-orange umbrella in her cocktail. 'Why are you doing this?'

'I don't want you to hide from me,' he said. 'I don't want you to play games. I hate it when you do that. I'm not going to exploit you. I'm not that sort of man. Surely you know that by now?'

Aiesha looked at him for a long moment. Everything about him was so incredibly special. His patience. His sensitivity. His kindness. Her heart felt so heavy at the thought of when this time together would be over. How would she ever find someone so in tune with her? How would she ever fill that giant hole of loneliness inside her once he was out of her life?

She took a little breath and slowly released it, her gaze going back to her drink. 'I hated everything about my childhood. I hated the poverty. I hated the cruelty.

I hated the fact I didn't fit in. For as long as I can remember, I dreamed of escaping. The only way I could escape was with music.'

'How did you learn to play the piano?' he asked. 'Did you have formal lessons?'

Aiesha kept looking at the tiny wooden spines on the umbrella. 'There was a piano in the church hall a block away from the estate we lived on. I used to go there and play it for hours. The pastor didn't seem to mind. After a while he started leaving a few music-theory books lying around. I taught myself to read music. The technique of playing was much harder to learn. I listened to CDs when I could but I'll never be good enough to play anywhere but a dingy nightclub.'

'But you play like a professional.'

She screwed up her mouth in a self-deprecating manner. 'I wouldn't be brave enough to play in front of a sober audience. Not my own stuff, that is.'

He leaned forward and took one of her hands in his. 'But you're so talented. That music you played the other day. It was so emotional, so haunting. It was like a soundtrack to a really emotional movie. Do you have more like that? Stuff you've written yourself?'

Aiesha looked at her hand in his. The engagement ring looked so real, so perfect for her finger. He was so perfect. Why had she taken this long to realise it? Or had she always realised it? He was perfect but she was wrong for him. Bad for him. She would bring trouble for him if she stayed around too long. Hadn't she caused enough trouble in the past? She brought her gaze up to his. 'You're nothing like him, you know.'

His brows met over his eyes. 'Who?'

'Your father.'

His expression clouded as he released her hand and sat back from her. 'I've spent too many years of my life trying to convince myself of that.'

'It's true, James.' She reached for his hand again, curling her fingers around his strong, capable ones. 'He doesn't care about anyone but himself. You care. Look at the way you looked after your mother after the divorce. She told me how you made sure she got a proper division of the assets. Your father would have swindled her out of her fair share but you stood up for her. You even paid the lawyer's bill. And you bought her Lochbannon. You visit her whenever you can. You worry about her hooking up with a guy you've never met. If that's not caring, I don't know what is.'

His mouth twisted as he looked down at their joined hands. 'I used to think my parents were doing OK. Not superhappy…but OK.' He looked at her again. 'I guess I didn't want to see my father for who he was. My mother, bless her for being so gracious, didn't want to ruin my relationship with him. But it cost her dearly. For year after year she put up with my father's affairs so I could have what she considered a normal upbringing. She came from a broken home and knew how hard it was for kids with shared custody arrangements.'

Aiesha stroked the length of his thumb where it was resting against her hand. 'It must have been a shock to finally find out the truth about him.'

'It was.' He flattened his mouth as if the memory disturbed him. 'I felt like my whole childhood was a lie. Everything I believed in was false. Love. Marriage. Commitment. It made me wonder if anyone was ever happy with their lot. That everyone was out there pretending to be OK when they were anything but.'

'I'm sure there are some people who get it right…' She looked at the way his thumb was now stroking the back of her hand. Her engagement ring—her fake engagement ring—glinted at her mockingly.

He turned her hand over in his, giving it a gentle squeeze. 'Want to dance?'

Aiesha slipped her arms around him as he drew her to her feet. She laid her head against his chest as he led her in a slow waltz on the small dance floor. Being in his arms felt safe. Made her feel anchored. Made her feel loved.

Loved?

James didn't love her. He cared about her. Like he cared about everybody. He was a responsible person who took others' welfare seriously. She would be a fool to conjure up one of her pointless little dreams. None of her dreams had ever come to life. None of her prayers had ever been answered. None of her planets had ever aligned.

James put his hand on the nape of her neck as he looked down at her. 'Where did you go just then?'

'Go?'

'You missed a step.'

'So? I'm a rubbish dancer.'

He held her gaze with the steadiness of his. 'No mask, remember?'

Aiesha chewed one side of her lower lip. 'This isn't easy for me...'

His thumb stroked where her teeth had been. 'I know it isn't.'

She looked at the knot of his tie. 'It's hard for me to let people get close. I push everyone away. I can't seem to help it.'

He cupped her cheek with his hand. 'Be yourself with me. Don't play games. Just be yourself.'

Aiesha looked into his dark eyes. 'I have nightmares. Horrible nightmares. About what happened to Archie. That's why I never share a bed with anyone. It's so embarrassing to wake up screaming or...or worse...' The truth came tumbling out in a rush but, instead of feeling ashamed, she felt relieved to have finally told him.

His eyes did that softening thing that melted her every time. 'Thank you,' he said.

'For what?'

His expression was full of tenderness, the sort of tenderness she had longed for someone to show her. 'For trusting me.'

Aiesha wondered if he knew how hard it was for her. She felt like someone had unzipped her wide open like a body bag. Everything was on show. Her doubts. Her fears. Her terrors. Her shame. But he wasn't repulsed. He wasn't pushing her away in disgust. He was looking at her with understanding and concern. Acceptance. She drew in a breath that rattled against the walls of her throat. 'How'd you get to be so nice with a father like yours?'

He gave her a twinkling smile. 'I can be bad when I need to be.'

She linked her arms around his neck and smiled back. 'Now that's something I'd like to see.'

James pulled the covers over Aiesha's sleeping form a few hours later. She was curled up like a kitten, her cheek pressed against the pillow next to his, her hair in a tumbled mass around her head. He stroked the wayward strands off her smooth brow, watching as her eyelids flickered in rapid-eye-movement sleep. She was so beautiful. So broken and yet so exquisitely beautiful it made his heart contract every time he looked at her.

Each time he made love with her he learned more about her. The way she expressed herself physically was an indication of the passionate emotion she kept hidden away. Was he fooling himself she felt something for him? How long would it take for her to feel safe enough to reveal her feelings to him? She had told him so much but not the words he most wanted to hear. He wanted to tell her how he felt but wondered if it was too soon. Would it spook her to have him reveal how deeply he cared?

She moved against him, snuggling up close, her eyes opening sleepily. 'What time is it?'

'Six a.m. Too early to get up.'

She rubbed one of her eyes with the ball of her fist, reminding him of a child waking up before it was ready. 'That's a big sleep-in for me.'

He took her balled-up fist and brought it to his mouth

and kissed the knuckle of her index finger. 'I liked having you beside me all night.'

Her expression faltered for a moment but then she gave him a slitted look from beneath her lashes. 'At least you didn't grope me.'

He rolled her on to her back and straddled her with his thighs. 'That was remiss of me. Is it too late to do it now?'

She laughed as he began to nuzzle her neck and he realised it was the first time he had heard her do so naturally. 'Stop it,' she said, batting him playfully with her fists. 'That tickles.'

He moved down to her breasts, kissing each one in turn. 'You don't really want me to stop, do you?'

She gave a little whimper as he moved down her belly. 'Not yet.'

'We could spend all day in bed,' he said. 'How does that sound?'

She gasped as he took a gentle nip of the tender flesh of her inner thigh. 'Don't you have terribly important work to do?'

He looked up and gave her a glinting smile. 'It can wait.'

When Aiesha entered the ballroom on James's arm later that evening, every eye turned to look at them as they walked to their designated table. All day, news feeds had run with the story of their engagement after the photos of them arriving at the hotel had gone around the world. Everyone was fascinated with the story of their romance. The former street kid and Vegas club singer

and the Old Money talented architect falling head over
heels in love. One journalist had even gone as far as
calling it a modern day re-enactment of *My Fair Lady.*

But that was exactly what it was like. She was act-
ing out a role in a play. She was dressed in the costume.
She had all the moves down pat. James was perfectly
cast as her leading man.

And tonight's event was their stage.

It was a highbrow affair with beautiful people
dressed impeccably, the women dripping with jewellery, the men dapper in bespoke tuxedos. As well kit-
ted out as Aiesha was in the black evening gown with
its mermaid train, she still felt like a little brown wood
duck surrounded by bright flamingos. She couldn't help
feeling that any minute now someone would tap her
on the shoulder and tell her to leave. Call her out for
a fake. Mock her for pretending to be something she
could never be.

She could see several women looking at her and ex-
changing comments behind their gloved hands. Were
they questioning James's sanity in choosing her? Were
they laughing at her behind their polite smiles? Nerves
fluttered in her stomach like moths with razor-blade
wings. What if she embarrassed James by doing or saying the wrong thing? What if she compromised his business deal? Hadn't she done enough damage to his name
and reputation?

James had his arm around her waist as he introduced
her to the host. 'Darling, this is Howard Sherwood.
Howard, my fiancée, Aiesha Adams.'

Howard smiled a smile that made his light blue eyes

twinkle as he took her hand. 'You're every bit as stunning as James said. Congratulations on your engagement. When's the big day?'

Aiesha felt a hot blush steal over her cheeks. Couldn't he see how much of an imposter she felt? She felt as if it was emblazoned on her forehead: FRAUD. 'Erm... we're still trying to sort out dates. We're both so crazily busy. You know how it is.'

'Well, don't leave it too long,' Howard said. 'Never was one for long engagements, or for living together for years on end. Waste of time. Might as well get on with it, eh, James? Make an honest woman out of her.'

James smiled an easy smile. 'That's the plan.'

Aiesha waited until Howard had turned to greet some other guests. 'You're becoming a rather accomplished liar. It's got me worried.'

His look was now unreadable. 'What would you like to drink?'

'Champagne.' She took a steadying breath as more and more people swarmed into the ballroom, stopping to take photos with their phones of her and James. 'Better make it a double.'

'According to the latest news feed, we're the new "it" couple,' he said as he handed her a bubbling glass of champagne.

'I can't imagine why. Quite frankly, I'm surprised everyone's bought it. Just shows how dumbed down people are these days to believe everything they read in the press.'

Aiesha drank half a glass of champagne before

she realised he was still standing staring at her with a frowning expression. 'What?'

He brushed an idle fingertip down her cheek, his dark blue eyes suddenly intense. Earnest. 'What if it was real?'

She swallowed. 'What if what was real?'

'Us.'

She flickered her eyelids. '*Us?*'

'We don't have to pretend,' he said. 'We could have a real relationship.'

Aiesha licked a layer of her lip gloss off her lips. Her heart was banging against her breastbone like a window shutter in a high wind. Air was not getting down into her lungs. Her throat was as restricted as a clogged drinking straw. He was joking. He had to be. He had got her to take off her armour and now he was playing her at her own game. Leading her on, flirting with her, making fun of her the way she had with him. She gave a little laugh but it sounded grating. 'Good one,' she said. 'You nearly had me there. Can you imagine what your father would say if you brought me home? He'd disinherit you on the spot. I'm surprised he hasn't already done it.'

James frowned at her, about to say something further but stopped himself.

'James, sorry to interrupt.' Howard Sherwood came over with a flustered look on his normally congenial face. 'There's been a problem with tonight's entertainment. The feature act has suddenly come down with a migraine. I just got the message from her agent.' He swung his gaze to Aiesha. 'Would you fill in for her,

Aiesha? James told me you're an entertainer. It'd just be for an hour till the dance band comes on.'

Aiesha's stomach pitched. 'I—I don't think—'

'Do it, darling,' James said. 'You'd be brilliant. Everyone will love you.'

'Please, Aiesha,' Howard said. 'You'd be doing my charity and me a massive favour. There are some big international sponsors here and they'll be disappointed if the programme is cut short. I'm happy to pay you if that's what's—'

'No, of course not,' Aiesha said. 'It's not about the money. I would do it for free but—'

'Wonderful.' Howard beamed and clapped James on the back. 'You've got a good woman there, James. Oh, and about that contract. Consider it done and dusted. I'm also going to recommend you to some colleagues in Argentina. Have you heard of the Valquez brothers Alejandro and Luis? They have a big hotel and resort expansion in the pipeline. It'll be worth squillions.'

Aiesha felt James's hand tighten around hers. Who hadn't heard of the Valquez brothers? They were two of the richest men in South America. How could she refuse to play now? It would mean so much to James to secure the Valquez contract. It would rebuild the Challender architecture empire back to what it had been in his grandfather's day and expand it even further. She took a deep breath as she pushed her cowardice and self-doubt behind her. 'When do you want me to start?'

James sat at the head table and watched as Aiesha played the first bracket. Her fingers were light over the keys, her voice a clear bell-like sound that made the hairs on his arms stand up. The song she was singing was an original of hers, the lyrics poignant and deeply moving. It was a song about lost dreams, lost love and heartbreak. The ballroom erupted into applause and then she deftly changed key and went into another song. This time it was about secret hopes and yearnings that spoke to something deep inside him. Her lyrics were so timely. Hadn't he been ignoring his own hopes and dreams? He had been fixated on working, rebuilding all that was lost in the scandal blow-out ten years ago, but he had neglected the emotional side of his life. He had shut down. Locked away his feelings. Ignored his feelings. Become an automaton. He had chosen a bride who would not make him feel anything other than mild affection.

Aiesha made him feel passion.

She made him feel alive.

She made him feel like a man who could take on the world.

He loved her. He knew it as certainly as he knew he was sitting there watching her win over the crowd. She was tugging on everyone's heartstrings. He could see women dabbing at the corners of their eyes with tissues. He could see grown men swallowing. Choking on suppressed emotion.

This was what she was meant to do. To sing like an angel, to play her music to make people feel in touch with their emotions. What a waste of her talent to sing to a disinterested audience in a lounge bar. Why hadn't he stepped in before and got her out of there? Hadn't she been crying out for help since she came home with his mother? He had turned his back on her. Rejected her, just like everyone else had done.

All that was going to change. He would ask her to marry him, this time without interruption. He would get down on bended knee and tell her how much he loved her. They would build a future together. Have a family together. The family she had missed out on. The family he would have loved to grow up with if things had been different.

He thought of their children, a little girl with sparkling grey eyes and a cheeky smile, or a little boy with a serious expression and dark blue eyes.

He wanted it all.

He wanted to make her happy. To make up for her miserable childhood, for all the disappointments and heartbreaks she had experienced.

He would be her knight in shining armour. He would be her Prince Charming. He would be her defender. Her protector. Her best friend and her lover. She would no longer have to fight her corner with that hard don't-mess-with-me look in her eyes.

He would make her feel safe.

He would make her feel loved.

Aiesha stood and took a bow after her performance was over. The applause was rapturous. She had never heard anything like it. She wanted to check behind her to see if they were clapping for someone else. Surely it couldn't be her they were applauding? She had played her own songs. Why? Because she hadn't wanted to bring any hint of Vegas showgirl into the ballroom. This was her one and only chance to show everyone what she was capable of.

She had played each composition with her heart behind every word and cadence. She had never done that before. Opened her heart fully to the music, to the audience. *To James.* She had used her music to reach across the room to tell him what she couldn't say in person. Hadn't had the courage to say when he spoke to her earlier. Was he serious about making their relationship real? What did he mean? Did he want to make it permanent? Had she imagined the earnestness in his dark blue gaze?

What did it matter whether he was earnest or not? She couldn't bring him down by continuing their relationship. How long before a living skeleton popped out of her family closet and brought more shame and embarrassment to him? Even more was at stake now. He had the Valquez deal to consider. Her background was never going to go away. It would always be there. There would always be a journalist unscrupulous enough to rake over her past. It was better to leave before the real damage was done. Before her hopes got too high. Before she dropped her guard low enough for James to see how she felt about him...

Cameras flashed and the room was abuzz as she made her way back to the table where James—along with everyone else—was giving her a standing ovation.

He gathered her in his arms and held her close. 'You were amazing, darling,' he said. 'Truly amazing.'

Aiesha gave a self-deprecating grimace. 'I missed

a key change in that first bracket. I hope there were no musos in the crowd. *So* amateur.'

He held her by the hands, looking at her with a thoughtful gaze. 'You're always doing that.'

'What?'

'Putting yourself down.'

'Yeah, well, best to get in first is my take on that.'

'Miss Adams?' A man came over with a business card in his hand. 'I'm George Bassleton. I'm a talent scout for a recording studio in London. I manage recording contracts for up-and-coming musicians. Would you be interested in coming into the studio for a sound test?'

Aiesha took the card with a hand that was close to shaking. 'I… Thank you.'

'You could be the next big thing in music,' George Bassleton said. 'The new Amy Winehouse or Norah Jones. You have a lot of soul in your voice. It's unique. Call me when you're back in London. I'll set something up.'

James smiled at her once the man had moved back to his own table. 'See? What did I tell you? You're a star in the making.'

She whooshed out a quick breath. 'You reckon I could slip out and take a breather for a minute? All this attention is going to my head.'

'Come on.' He took her by the hand. 'I know just the place.'

Aiesha followed him to a quiet alcove behind a huge flower arrangement where two velvet-covered chairs and a small brass-inlaid drum table were situated. James had organised a waiter to bring an ice bucket and champagne as well as a long, cool mineral water with a twist of lime. He waited until she had drained the mineral water before he got down on bended knee in front of her chair. 'What are you doing?' she said, glancing around the legs of her chair. 'Have you lost something down there?'

He took her hands in his. 'I almost did lose something. You.'

Aiesha chewed at her dust-dry lips. Time to get the mask back on, even if it didn't feel as comfortable as it used to. 'Hey, I know my music is a tad sentimental and all that but you're really spooking me. It looks like you're about to propose to me, which would be a really dumb thing to do for a guy in your situation.'

His brows came together. 'Why?'

She gave one of her tinny laughs. 'You and me? Are you nuts? We'd kill each other before the honeymoon was over. Nice proposal, though.'

His hands gripped hers. 'Aiesha, I love you. I'm not sure when I started loving you. It just…happened. I want to marry you. I mean it. This isn't a joke or a set-up. I'm serious. I want you to be my wife.'

Aiesha got to her feet, almost knocking him off balance in the process. 'But here's the thing. I don't love you.'

He got to his feet and took her firmly by the shoulders. 'That's a lie. You *do* love me. I see it in your eyes. I feel it when we make love. You love me but you're too scared to say it because, hell, I don't know why. Maybe you've never had anyone love you before. But *I* love you. My mother loves you. You're the woman I've been waiting for all my life.'

Aiesha wanted to say it. She *ached* to say it. But the words were trapped in her chest. Years of heartbreak and disappointment and crushed hopes had buried them so deep she couldn't access them. She had loved her mother. She had loved Archie. But both had been ripped away from her, tearing her heart out of her chest each time, leaving a gaping, empty hole that still pulsed and throbbed with pain.

It was better to get out now while she still could. James would get over it. He would find some other girl from his nice, neat, ordered world.

'I'm sorry, James.' She steeled her gaze and iced what remained of her heart. 'Believe me, it's for the best. You're a nice guy and all that, but you're *too* nice. I'm already feeling bored.'

His frown was so heavy it closed the distance between his glittering eyes. 'I don't believe you. You want what I want. I know you do. Why won't you admit it?'

'Let's not make a scene,' she said. 'It wouldn't be good for your image. Howard Sherwood might change his mind about recommending you to his posh polo-playing pals.'

'Do you think I give a freaking toss for that?' he said. 'It's you I care about. I'd give it all up for you. All of it.'

Aiesha wondered if he knew how close he would be to losing it all if she stayed in his life. No one wanted bad blood. Not in their family. Not in their social circle. Not in their business dealings. What would happen to his squillion-dollar deal if her father or stepfather gave a tell-all interview to the press? She was surprised one or both hadn't already done so. There was money in it. Big money. The shame would be back in James's life. Shame she had brought in like dirty baggage. She couldn't escape her past. It would always be there like a horrible spectre just waiting for the worst possible moment to appear. 'I'm going to the powder room,' she said. 'I'll meet you back in the ballroom. We can talk about this later.'

His eyes took on a cynical hardness. 'You think I'm that stupid? You're going to run away as soon as I turn my back. That's what cowards do, Aiesha. I thought you were stronger than that. Tougher. Seems I was wrong.'

She stood straight and tall and determined before him. 'I'm not a coward.' *I'm doing this for you. Can't you see that?* 'Don't you *dare* call me a coward.'

'Go on, then,' he said through tightened lips. 'Go. Run away from what frightens you. See how far you get before you realise you've run away from everything that matters to you.'

'*You* don't matter to me, James,' she said with feigned cold, hard indifference. 'Your money matters to me. It's all I ever wanted from you or any man.' She put on her bad-girl smirk. 'Maybe I could look up your father. At least I'm legal now. Do you have his number?'

His jaw worked for a moment, his eyes turning blue-black with disgust. 'Find it yourself.' And, with that, he turned on his heel and left.

CHAPTER TWELVE

Two weeks later...

JAMES LOOKED AT his phone for the fiftieth time. No missed calls. No text messages. He knew he was being stubborn in refusing to reach out to Aiesha. But he wanted her to stop the game playing. He should never have fallen for that crack about his father. Of course she wouldn't contact his father—he was too busy sunning himself on the beach at an exclusive resort in Barbados with not one, but two girls half his age.

James pushed a hand through his hair. Even his mother was having a better love life than him. She was holidaying with Richard in outback Australia, camping under the stars while he was sitting here brooding over the one that got away.

The press had done their thing over his broken engagement with Aiesha. The speculation had been excruciating but he had done his best to ignore it. He had more important things to worry about. He wanted Aiesha to come to him. To reach out to him. He had offered her his heart and she had tossed it aside like a toy she had finished playing with.

Had he got it wrong about her? Had she been playing him for a fool the whole time? He thought of the way they had made love. Surely he hadn't imagined that once-in-a-lifetime intimacy. What about the way she had told him of her worst nightmares and fears? She had opened herself to him in a way she had never done to anyone else. He was sure of it. He *knew* her. He *loved* her.

He pushed back from his desk with a muttered curse. How long was this going to take? He was a patient man but this was getting way past ridiculous. He missed her. He ached to be with her, especially now as her career was about to take off. He'd read about her recording contract in the press. She had her first concert tonight in Berlin as a supporting act for a big-name band who was on a comeback tour. It was massive exposure for her. According to what he'd gathered from the press, if tonight was a success she would be joining the band on the rest of their world tour.

His phone flashed on the desk with an incoming message. He snatched it up but when he looked at the screen it wasn't a text, but a news feed coming through on social media. His gut clenched when he read through the article that had been tweeted. Aiesha's stepfather had given a warts-and-all interview to the press. It was nothing but a pack of lies. It disgusted him to read such trash about someone he loved so much. And of course the journalist had taken it one step further by including photos of his father and Aiesha's role in his parents' divorce.

There was even a photo of her biological father outside the court where he had been sentenced to prison. The shame of it might derail her on her big night. Who would be there to protect her from the fallout? Who would be there to comfort her? To stop her having a meltdown in case it all got too much?

He clicked on his computer screen to bring up a flight booking.

He would.

'Miss Adams?' The events manager, Kate Greenhill, popped her head around the dressing room door at the concert hall in Berlin. 'You're on in five minutes.'

Aiesha adjusted her droplet earrings, trying to fight the ants' nest of nerves in her belly. She would have to get used to this if she was asked to join the rest of the tour. Nerves. Panic. Doubt. What if she missed a note? What if her voice froze? What if the audience hated her? 'Thanks, Kate. What's the crowd like?'

Kate grinned at her in the light bulb-lined mirror. 'Massive. A sell-out. To be honest, I think they're here to hear you, not the band. The boys won't be too happy about that. This is supposed to be their come-back chance.'

Aiesha knew she should be feeling satisfied. Proud of what she had achieved in spite of all the setbacks in her life. She had been booked as the supporting act for the opening concert of the band's reunion tour. She had an album in production. She had the prospect of fans. Fame. Fortune.

But she was lonely.

Desperately, achingly lonely.

James hadn't contacted her. Not once. She knew it was for the best. He had to distance himself from her, especially now. Her stepfather had finally sold his story to the press. She suspected he had waited until now so he could go for collateral damage. He couldn't have timed it better. The lurid tale of her being a smart-mouthed teenage tease who had tried to seduce him had gone viral. The press had subsequently sourced photos from all over the place. It had stirred up renewed interest in the scandal with James's father, which would cause enormous embarrassment and hurt to Louise and James. There was even a photo of Aiesha's father being led out of court on the day he was sentenced.

Lovely. Just lovely.

Her business manager/publicist assured her that any publicity was good while she was building her career as a solo artist, but Aiesha wasn't so sure. She wanted to distance herself from her past. She wanted to be known for her music, not for her dodgy bloodline or step-relatives or her past behaviour. It would be different if she were a rock-and-roll chick. But she wasn't. She was a love-song and ballad singer with a hint of blues and jazz.

Louise Challender had sent her roses and a sweet message. Aiesha had held the card against her chest and cried so much the make-up artist had hysterics.

The card said: 'I always knew you would make it. Love you, Louise.'

But she hadn't made it. Not yet. Maybe not ever if the news of her past kept resurfacing like a bad smell at a perfume launch.

Kate popped her head back around the door. 'Two minutes.'

Aiesha let out a rattling breath. She hadn't done her vocal warm-up. She hadn't focused. She wasn't prepared. This was not how she'd thought it would be. She loved writing songs; she loved being in the recording studio working with the team to produce the best tracks she could. But singing her songs in front of huge crowds was not the thrill she'd thought it would be. What was the point of singing those heartfelt words when the only person she wanted to hear them wasn't in the audience?

The crowd roared as Aiesha came out to the spotlight, the beam so strong she could only make out the faces in the first few rows. She sat down at the piano, took a deep breath and went into the routine she had planned with her agent.

But then, towards the end of her performance, she turned on the piano stool and trained her gaze to the sea of unseen faces at the back. 'This song is a new one. No one has heard it before now.' She blinked to stem a sudden rush of tears. 'It's called "The Love I Had to Let Go."'

The roar when the song was over was deafening. Aiesha got up from the piano and took a bow. She had three standing ovations. As she performed each follow-up song she kept reminding herself: *This is what you wanted. This is your moment. You've wanted this since you were five years old. Enjoy it, for pity's sake.*

It was supposed to be the triumph of her life. But as she walked back through the bowels of the stage set to her dressing room she felt empty…like a deflated balloon at a children's party. Useless.

Kate came in while Aiesha was taking off her make-up. 'Um, there's someone here to see you.'

Aiesha put the discarded facial wipe in the bin next to her chair. 'I told you before. I'm not doing any press interviews.'

'He's not a journalist,' Kate said.

Aiesha swivelled to look at her. 'Who is it?'

'It's me,' James said from the door.

Aiesha swallowed. Put her hand on her stomach to stop it from falling even further. 'Erm…would you leave us for a minute, Kate? This won't take long.'

'Sure.' Kate smiled brightly. 'Nice to meet you, Mr Challender.'

'You, too, Kate.'

The silence was as deafening as the applause had been only a few minutes ago.

Aiesha rolled her lips together, searching for something to say. 'You should've told me you were coming. I could've got you complimentary tickets.'

His dark blue eyes held hers in an unreadable lock. 'You know me. I don't mind paying.'

Her cheeks still had a layer of bronzer on them but, even so, she was sure he would know she was blushing. 'So, what brings you here? Did you have business in Berlin? It's a lovely city, isn't it? I've always wanted to come here. It's weird because now I'm here I can't walk down the street without worrying someone will recognise me from the tour poster.' She was talking too much but at least it filled that ghastly silence. 'That's the price you pay for fame, huh?'

'Is it everything you hoped for?'

She painted on a smile. 'You would not believe the amount of money in my bank account. Oh, that reminds me.' She turned and fished in her bag in the drawer under the make-up counter. 'Ah, here it is. I knew I had it somewhere.' She held the engagement ring out to him in her open palm and stretched her smile a little further. 'I can buy my own jewellery now.'

He ignored the ring. 'How are you?'

'I'm fine. And you?'

'I see your stepfather sold a pack of lies to the press,' he said.

'Yes, I've been expecting that for a while now. It'll keep him in drink and cigarettes and drugs for a year or two.'

'Are you going to do anything about it?'

She shrugged. 'What can I do? Hopefully, it will blow away in a day or two.'

His brow was deeply furrowed. 'But it could damage your reputation before you get your career properly launched. You're only starting out. It could destroy what you've worked so hard for.'

Aiesha closed her fingers over the ring, barely noticing how it bit into the flesh of her palm. 'You shouldn't be here, James. People will talk.'

'So? Let them talk.'

'Your business will suffer.' She dropped the ring on the counter next to her make-up kit, turning her back on him as she straightened the cosmetic brushes in a neat line. 'Your reputation has a lot further to fall than mine. It could jeopardise your business.'

He let out an expletive and spun her around to face

him. 'Is that why you fed me that rubbish about not loving me?'

Aiesha looked into his glittering eyes. Tears were not far away in hers. They didn't look far away in his, either. 'Don't make this any harder for me. I don't belong in your life. I don't belong in your world. I'll bring you down, James. I'll ruin everything for you. It's already happening all over again.'

He pulled her up and crushed her to his chest. 'You silly little goose.' He kissed the top of her head, the side of her face, her chin, her nose and then finally a hot, hard kiss on her mouth. He held her from him, his eyes misty. 'That song. That was for me, wasn't it? I was the love you had to let go.'

Aiesha could barely speak for the emotions that were rising like a tsunami in her chest. A huge, emotional storm that was like a cauldron boiling over. 'I didn't want to hurt you. I figured I'd already hurt you enough. Letting you go was the hardest thing I've ever had to do.'

'I love you.' His hands gripped her shoulders so tightly it was close to pain but she didn't care. 'I love you so much. It's been so hard to stay away from you. Every day I wanted to call you. To beg you to come back to me.'

'Why did you come now?' Aiesha said. 'Why not before?'

'I was angry after what happened in Paris,' he said. 'But I stubbornly refused to make the first move, even though I realised soon after you'd only made that crack about hooking up with my father as a way to push me away.'

She gave him a sheepish look. 'I'm sorry about that. It was a pretty crass thing to say.'

He cupped her face in his hands. 'When that awful story came out this morning, I was sick with worry. I was worried there would be no one by your side to protect you. I want to be that person, Aiesha. I want to make you feel safe. I want you to feel loved. I want you to feel accepted. You're a part of me. I can't function without you. Just ask my mother. She's been tearing her hair out over me. You can't do that to her. You have to marry me, otherwise she'll never speak to me again. How bad would that be? You would have cost her a husband *and* a son.'

Aiesha felt a smile break open her face. It unlocked something gnarled and tightly bound inside her chest. 'I guess when you put it that way, how could I refuse?'

His hands tightened again on her shoulders. 'You mean it? You'll marry me?'

She laughed at his shocked expression. 'Aren't you going to ask me to say it?'

'Say what?'

'The three little magic words.'

He grinned as he pulled her close again. 'I heard you the first time.'

She wrinkled her brow as she tilted her head back to look at him. 'When was that?'

'On stage tonight,' he said. 'You turned to the audience and I knew you were speaking directly to me. I sat and cried like a baby through that song. I was surrounded by thousands of people and yet I felt like I was the only one in the audience.'

Aiesha blinked through tears of happiness. 'That's because you're the only one that matters to me.'

His eyes twinkled. 'What about my money?'

She twinkled her eyes right on back. 'I've got my own money.'

'What about my mother? She matters to you, doesn't she?'

Aiesha felt a warm rush of love flow through her. 'You know she does.'

'Have you ever told her?'

'Not in so many words, but I think she knows.'

He stroked her cheeks with his thumbs. 'You could call her and tell her. I think she'd love to hear you say the words. She's ridiculously sentimental like that.'

Aiesha put her arms around his neck. 'I want you to hear them first. I never said them to anyone else before.' She looked him in the eyes, her heart suddenly feeling too big for her chest. 'I love you.'

His eyes watered up. His throat moved up and down. His arms around her tightened. 'I love you, too. So much. I never thought it was possible to love someone this much. You will marry me, won't you?'

She gave him a teasing smile. 'I wonder if anyone's ever accepted a marriage proposal in a dressing room before?'

He brought his mouth down to within a millimetre of hers. 'First time for everything,' he said, and then he kissed her.

* * * * *

Mills & Boon® Hardback
July 2014

ROMANCE

Christakis's Rebellious Wife	Lynne Graham
At No Man's Command	Melanie Milburne
Carrying the Sheikh's Heir	Lynn Raye Harris
Bound by the Italian's Contract	Janette Kenny
Dante's Unexpected Legacy	Catherine George
A Deal with Demakis	Tara Pammi
The Ultimate Playboy	Maya Blake
Socialite's Gamble	Michelle Conder
Her Hottest Summer Yet	Ally Blake
Who's Afraid of the Big Bad Boss?	Nina Harrington
If Only...	Tanya Wright
Only the Brave Try Ballet	Stefanie London
Her Irresistible Protector	Michelle Douglas
The Maverick Millionaire	Alison Roberts
The Return of the Rebel	Jennifer Faye
The Tycoon and the Wedding Planner	Kandy Shepherd
The Accidental Daddy	Meredith Webber
Pregnant with the Soldier's Son	Amy Ruttan

MEDICAL

200 Harley Street: The Shameless Maverick	Louisa George
200 Harley Street: The Tortured Hero	Amy Andrews
A Home for the Hot-Shot Doc	Dianne Drake
A Doctor's Confession	Dianne Drake

Mills & Boon® Large Print

July 2014

ROMANCE

A Prize Beyond Jewels	Carole Mortimer
A Queen for the Taking?	Kate Hewitt
Pretender to the Throne	Maisey Yates
An Exception to His Rule	Lindsay Armstrong
The Sheikh's Last Seduction	Jennie Lucas
Enthralled by Moretti	Cathy Williams
The Woman Sent to Tame Him	Victoria Parker
The Plus-One Agreement	Charlotte Phillips
Awakened By His Touch	Nikki Logan
Road Trip with the Eligible Bachelor	Michelle Douglas
Safe in the Tycoon's Arms	Jennifer Faye

HISTORICAL

The Fall of a Saint	Christine Merrill
At the Highwayman's Pleasure	Sarah Mallory
Mishap Marriage	Helen Dickson
Secrets at Court	Blythe Gifford
The Rebel Captain's Royalist Bride	Anne Herries

MEDICAL

Her Hard to Resist Husband	Tina Beckett
The Rebel Doc Who Stole Her Heart	Susan Carlisle
From Duty to Daddy	Sue MacKay
Changed by His Son's Smile	Robin Gianna
Mr Right All Along	Jennifer Taylor
Her Miracle Twins	Margaret Barker

Mills & Boon® Hardback
August 2014

ROMANCE

Zarif's Convenient Queen	Lynne Graham
Uncovering Her Nine Month Secret	Jennie Lucas
His Forbidden Diamond	Susan Stephens
Undone by the Sultan's Touch	Caitlin Crews
The Argentinian's Demand	Cathy Williams
Taming the Notorious Sicilian	Michelle Smart
The Ultimate Seduction	Dani Collins
Billionaire's Secret	Chantelle Shaw
The Heat of the Night	Amy Andrews
The Morning After the Night Before	Nikki Logan
Here Comes the Bridesmaid	Avril Tremayne
How to Bag a Billionaire	Nina Milne
The Rebel and the Heiress	Michelle Douglas
Not Just a Convenient Marriage	Lucy Gordon
A Groom Worth Waiting For	Sophie Pembroke
Crown Prince, Pregnant Bride	Kate Hardy
Daring to Date Her Boss	Joanna Neil
A Doctor to Heal Her Heart	Annie Claydon

MEDICAL

Tempted by Her Boss	Scarlet Wilson
His Girl From Nowhere	Tina Beckett
Falling For Dr Dimitriou	Anne Fraser
Return of Dr Irresistible	Amalie Berlin

4GEN STD HB

Mills & Boon® Large Print

August 2014

ROMANCE

HISTORICAL

MEDICAL

Discover more romance at

www.millsandboon.co.uk

- ❤ WIN great prizes in our exclusive competitions

- ❤ BUY new titles before they hit the shops

- ❤ BROWSE new books and REVIEW your favourites

- ❤ SAVE on new books with the Mills & Boon® Bookclub™

- ❤ DISCOVER new authors

PLUS, to chat about your favourite reads, get the latest news and find special offers:

- Find us on facebook.com/millsandboon
- Follow us on twitter.com/millsandboonuk
- ❤ Sign up to our newsletter at millsandboon.co.uk